SPLITSCREEN ENTERTAINMENT

Zombie Tube

A Nerdy Adventure

Mike Mankoff

3/11/2012

Zombie Tube: A Nerdy Adventure

This book is a work of fiction. Any resemblance to any persons living or dead is purely coincidental. Please don't sue me, I don't have any money.

Romeoville, IL.

Mankoff, Michael.

Zombie Tube.

ISBN- 978-0-615-61571-4

To my wife Janet.

Contents

"Ask me about my zombie plan."—Rooster Teeth T-Shirt

"Be nice to nerds. Chances are you'll end up working for one."—Bill Gates

"I want to put a ding in the universe" – Steve Jobs

"Use your head; cut off theirs."— Max Brooks, *The Zombie Survival Guide*

Prologue

There is less security in the White House than you think. I am not talking about the parts that bored school children walk around in, pretending to pay attention to their teachers but actually searching for a nearby fire alarm to pull. I am talking about the part of the White House that no one ever sees. This part of the White House, which everyone there calls "The Office," is located underneath the building. You can only get in after showing a rather severe looking black secret service agent named Phil your I.D. badge. Once Phil clears you, you get on the elevator and go in.

The Office looks pretty much like any other standard office building. The walls are painted an off white, and pictures of flowers and mountains dot the halls. Women in skirts and high heels struggle to walk while they carry documents from room to room. Men who smell like overpriced cologne sit in expensive business suits and make comments to each other about the legs on the women wearing the skirts, and the women pretend not to notice.

A typical American office, except for Phil outside the elevator. But it is in this office that almost all the important decisions get made. It is where the interns making $10/hr hunch over small desks editing speeches and analyzing data. It makes sense though. Who could forge a treaty when just outside the door a group of middle school bullies are stuffing a kid into a desk drawer?

As I had been let out of the Center for Disease Control early that morning, I arrive at the meeting room well before the appointed time. The conference room has a projector, already on and projecting eerie yellow light onto a white screen. A giant wooden conference table dominates the middle of the room. In the middle of the table is a small piece of computer equipment, a flat disk about a foot long. Over the equipment stands a long haired brunette, frowning and fiddling with wires connected to it. She is wearing a black sleeveless shirt with a gray skirt and nylons. Concentrating on her work, she doesn't see me enter the room and continues to frown in frustration. I stand and admire her for a bit, because she is incredibly beautiful, and I haven't seen any women not wearing a white lab coat and carrying a needle in three months. Her face breaks into dazzling smile, showing perfect white teeth over red lipstick. She hits a button on the flat disk and says, "Ok, Frank, can you hear me now?"

The box in the center of the room squawks a gruff, "Yes." A click announces the end of the call.

Giggling, the girl says, "Good," in a halfway decent impression of that Verizon guy. Mumbling under her breath about finally getting lunch, she looks up and notices me. Looking me up and down, she brushes hair out of her eyes. A tattoo sits on her forearm, just under her right hand. It is a tribal circle with glyphs in the middle. I recognize the glyphs as being Elfish, although I don't know what they mean. I am so caught up in the tattoo and the stirring in my loins that when she asks me who I am and what I am doing standing in this room staring at her, I blurt, "What does your tattoo say?"

She answers in a monotone voice that tells me that she is tired of explaining the tattoo. "It's Elfish, and it's my sister's name. And yes, that's elfish as in elves with pointy ears. "

"They live in trees and worship all things earthen. They are incredibly beautiful." I do my best to stare at her intently. I try to channel James Bond, but I fear that it comes across more like plain old Malcolm.

She blushes a bit, looking down and brushing more hair over her ear. "Most people don't react like that."

"Well, I am not most people." Ok, so as a writer, I know that is a cheesy line, but it works. She looks at me again with intriguing brown eyes. We are silent for a time, so to break the awkward silence I ask, "So, <u>Lord of the Rings</u> elves or <u>Inheritance Cycle</u> elves?"

"Either, although I think that the elves from <u>Inheritance</u> are a bit more badass than the elves from <u>Lord of the Rings</u>. But back to the original question, who are you, and what are you doing here?" This time when she asks, she is not as suspicious and has a half smile on her face that makes me want to rush up and hold her.

"I'm Malcolm. I'm the reason you're in here setting up that phone and projector instead of eating lunch. Sorry about that." All vestiges of James Bond disappear. I am a geeky kid in High School again.

She stops and looks me up and down once more. "Malcolm as in Malcolm Tushton? The guy who made all the zombie movies on the internet?"

I want to give credit where credit is due because I wasn't making those movies alone. This girl, however, is incredibly pretty, and knows who I am. I shrug and offer her my hand. "That's me."

I expect her to ask me if I know Ackmed, the good looking one, but she takes my hand and says, "I'm Sam. Sorry that I didn't recognize you. I am so embarrassed because I am such a huge fan. The writing on those internet shows was fantastic. I wish that I could write like that. "

She holds my hand just a couple of seconds longer than necessary. This close to me, I can smell her perfume. She smells good, a combination of cherry and sugar wound together to achieve a distinctly feminine essence. Fighting the urge to tell her how nice she smells, I thank her. I love it when a chick recognizes good writing. The elfish tattoo doesn't hurt either.

"So how does an internet writer come to be in a room with a projector and a phone connection directly wired to the Department of Defense?"

I invite her to sit in one of the big leather office chairs around the table, enjoying the view of her legs before they disappear. "It all began last May at Big Choice computers."

****

Mr. Humphrey stands in front of me yelling. He is about 40 years old and Indian, but with no accent, just dark skin and a pot belly. He has been yelling at me about his computer for nearly twenty minutes. Spittle forms in the corner of his mouth and flies at me every minute or two, giving me a slimy, curry scented shower. When he finally pauses for a breath, I tell him, "Sir, I know that you wanted your computer back, but the service is not complete yet."

In reality, the computer is finished and sitting in the metal cabinet behind me. All I had to do was remove some viruses the guy got from looking at porn. According to his browser history, he has a penchant for male strippers getting fucked by the girls watching them strip. It's called CFNM, and Mr. Humphrey's browsing history told me a sad tale about how often he indulged in such videos. When he brought the computer in, he wasted no time telling me how important he was and how soon he expected his service to be finished. I was going to hold it in service for another day, but his current tirade has annoyed me. I decide that it will be at least another week before he gets to watch more strippers.

As I am explaining to him how hard it is to service a laptop, my friend Ackmed walks up holding a laptop box in his arms. He is followed by a stunning blonde woman. She is about 20 years old. Tall and muscular, with dark skin and long dark hair, Ackmed resembles Naveen Andrews. He says something to the blonde, who giggles. While Mr. Humphrey continues to tell me what a loser I am for jockeying a counter at Big Choice computers so late into my 20's, I admire the girl's white legs and jean shorts. Ackmed whispers something into her ear and she giggles again. She sounds kind of like a stereotype of a cheerleader; ditzy. Perfect for Ackmed.

Mr. Humphrey continues to rant and Ackmed begins making faces at me. Mr. Humphrey can't see Ackmed, but the sight makes me have to look away to keep from cracking up. Out of the corner of my eye, I see my other friend Kevin taping the exchange with one of our store cameras. He pans the camera to make sure that he gets every ounce of Mr. Humphrey's spittle in stunning HD.

The girl laughs so hard at Ackmed that even Mr. Humphrey turns around to see what is going on behind him. Noticing her beauty, he looks quickly at the ground like a shy 16 year old boy lost in the girls' locker room. Mumbling something to me about next week, Mr. Humphrey walks away quickly, never looking up from the ground. Ackmed ushers the girl to my counter and tells me that she has just bought a computer and would like me to set it up. It's a relatively easy job, so I tell her that I will have it done in about an hour. Smiling, she walks away to pay. Ackmed winks at me, and I know that he will thank me later for both for the sale and for the quick service; both will, no doubt, help him secure the blonde's phone number. If I can't get laid myself, I can at least live vicariously through my good looking friends.

The laptop really just needs to have some information entered in it, but I do the girl a favor and delete Norton Internet Security so that it will run quickly. Since she was cute, I also run PC Decrappifier to get rid of all the extra software. As I work, Kevin and I debate the merits of different laptop brands while he plays with the camera he is still holding. I am still deleting proprietary software when I hear a groan. Glancing up, I see dark skin. "Mr. Humphrey, I told you that the laptop is not going to be ready for a couple of weeks."

Kevin mumbles something about looking at porn elsewhere as he slowly spins around, focusing and unfocusing the camera. I hear a groan again, and finally look up. It's Mr. Humphrey standing in front of me; only he is different now. His throat has been torn open, and there is blood on his white shirt. His face is now more gray than brown and his eyes are dead. He moans and reaches for me. Backing up, I say, "Kevin," loud enough to get his attention. Kevin, still looking through the video camera, begins to apologize for his porn comment, but stops when he sees Mr. Humphrey.

"Holy shit," he cries, backing up and simultaneously swinging the camera to record. "That's a fucking zombie."

As if I need to be told that the man in front of me is a zombie. I have read Max Brooks.

I begin to move around our counter. I hear screams erupt from the other side of the store. "Let's get out of here."

People around us are beginning to notice Mr. Humphrey, who moves away from us and attacks a fat guy with glasses holding a computer case. While his attention is diverted, Kevin and I run towards the door. We meet Ackmed near the cashers table. He is standing on top of it, kicking at the blonde girl that bought the laptop. She is reaching up for him with bloody hands.

Kevin sounds oddly calm. "What happened? "

"I don't know." Ackmed moves and kicks the girl in the face, but she doesn't seem to notice. "She walked out and was fine, but then she came back like this. "

"I think she's a zombie." Kevin regards her curiously, like a biology professor studying a new type of frog.

"I don't care what she is; just get her away from me before I get bitten." Ackmed again kicks the girl. The kick causes her to back up a few feet, but she instantly walks back towards him as if she didn't even feel it.

"You certainly have a way with women," I tell him, looking for a weapon. Nothing jumps out at me, and I wish for a few seconds that I worked somewhere with better weapons. Like a gun store. Or the Army. The only thing I can find is a toy lightsaber put near the checkout counter to encourage impulse buying and give little kids something to whine about while they wait in line.

Opening the lightsaber packaging, which reads, Makes Realistic Star Wars Sounds, I extend the lightsaber to its full three feet in length. It is made of cheap green plastic. Ackmed, sounding panicked, asks, "A plastic lightsaber?"

I ignore him and hit the woman as hard as I can. The lightsaber makes a realistic electronic whooshing sound as I swing it over my head. For a second, I really do feel like Luke Skywalker. To my dismay, the plastic lightsaber cracks and I am left holding a cheap lightsaber handle that continues to emit lightsaber noises.

Fuck George Lucas and his shitty toys.

I am not sure if it is me hitting her or the sounds coming from the hilt, but the blonde turns towards me, revealing a face that is half covered with blood and gore. She isn't so pretty now, but she is probably still smarter than some of the girls Ackmed has slept with. With no other option, I wave the broken lightsaber, which whooshes accordingly. The blonde follows it with her eyes like a dog staring at a bone. I throw the useless hilt as far as I can and scream, "Fetch." To my utter amazement, she limps after the toy, allowing us to escape outside into a brand new nightmare.

The parking lot already looks like a scene from Mad Max or any other generic apocalypse movie. People run around screaming, desperate to get to safety. Cars going far too fast drive through the lot, all vying to get to the street as quickly as possible. A black Camero swerves to avoid a gray pickup truck, hitting a curb and flipping into the air. The Camero slides on its roof into the door of the Old Navy store located next to Big Choice, sparks appearing as the metal hood scraps the concrete. We brace ourselves for an explosion. I guess that cars only explode in the movies, because this car just sits with its front half embedded in Old Navy's sliding glass doors, wheels still spinning. The man driving it screams for help, and is rewarded as two zombies appear from inside the store. Both wear khakis and collared shirts, and appear to be fashionable. They must be employees, because they also wear the stupid headsets that Old Navy hands out to its staff. Like anything that ever happens at Old Navy is so important it has to be dealt with immediately. As the two self important zombies growl, the man in the car screams louder. The pair of well dressed zombies attempt to get into the car, but can't seem to figure out how to open the door. They stand howling and scratching at the flipped vehicle, adding their cries to the now frantic screams of the man trapped inside.

A man wearing a camouflage hat and driving a pickup truck with an NRA sticker on it slams on his brakes as an old woman slowly backs a minivan out of a parking spot. As the man begins to curse at the woman, she calmly exits her vehicle and shoots him in the face. Getting back into her minivan, she waves at us and drives away.

On the ground near us, a man lays bleeding from his neck, moaning softly. He tries to staunch the blood with his hands, but his breathing becomes ragged and quick as blood continues to pour through his fingers. Suddenly, he stops moaning and tenses up. His eyes close, and his muscles relax. He lookes peaceful for a second, then his eyes open. Moaning again, although this time sounding far more menacing, he begins to crawl towards us, arms outstretched.

"They must turn into zombies after they die." Kevin sounds intrigued.

I point at the man with one hand and try to sound as bored as I can. "No shit. They're zombies."

Ackmed spots my green 1997 Chevy Lumina and begins walking towards it. "That's great, let's not stick around to find out more."

We manage to make it to the car, and after performing some awesome driving moves that I learned in Grand Theft Auto 3, I pull out of the parking lot and into the street.

∎∎

The streets are in bad shape, with lots of accidents and cars containing panicked drivers haphazardly swerving in and out of traffic at high speeds. Most of the people driving the cars can't handle the speed, so most of them careen out of control and strike other cars. Luckily for me though, I went through a racing game phase when I was 14. I had the full steering wheel from Sony, complete with a gas and brake pedal. The phase passed when I learned to drive a real car a couple of years later, but I still possess mad racing skills.

I swerve the Chevy violently left to avoid the twisted remains of a smashed Caravan. Kevin is white as a ghost. "Did that just happen? "

I smile to try to calm him down. "It just happened. Ackmed got turned down in a big way by that blonde. And I am a fucking amazing driver."

Ackmed observes the chaos flying by his window. "Funny."

Kevin puts his head in his hands. "We are living in the zombie apocalypse."

"Well, if anyone can survive, it's us. We seemed to do pretty well in the store." Ackmed sounds upbeat, and I agree. We had done well in the store. Maybe I could be a success in the zombie apocalypse. I might even be able to get laid easier.

Kevin seems overwhelmed. "Jesus, the whole fucking world is gone. No more Coffee."

Coffee is Kevin's latest crush. She works at Big Choice as a cashier. She knows nothing about video games, but has a dazzling smile and perky breasts. Kevin brings her a latte every morning and all she gives him is a smile. He's better off without Coffee. Still, he is upset. "I am sure it's not the whole world. We have got to lay low and hide out until this gets fixed. Someone will stop it."

He doesn't look convinced. As we narrowly miss a silver Mercedes that is smoking, I continue. "It can't be the apocalypse. Skyrim doesn't come out for another month, and I want really want to play it."

It is a logical fallacy, but at that point, I am looking for anything to make me appear calmer than I feel. Although I might get laid more in the zombie apocalypse, I also have begun to get a bit afraid. Coffee is gone. And there is no Skyrim.

"You haven't even finished all of Oblivion yet. And did you ever finish Morrowind, or go back and play any of the others? What about Fallout, man? It's the same game as Oblivion, only with guns."

I counter that Fallout was buggy, and Oblivion was Bethsada's crowning achievement. And I had finished the whole thing, even the Knights of the Nine expansions.

"It's pronounced Bethesda, like the city. And Fallout is better." Kevin appears to have lost himself in the world of video games and is noticeably calmer. He takes his hands from his face and points an accusing finger at me.

"We need to get to my parents," Ackmed announces. It is not a question; it is a statement of fact. My parents are vacationing in Hawaii, and Kevin's are dead. The only other people in the area that we care about are Ackmed's parents. Still, it is unnerving that I have just helped Kevin calm down, only to have Ackmed go all serious on me.

Kevin pats Ackmed's shoulder. "Sure man, that's fine. We are almost back to Lemont anyway."

Lemont is a small town of about 10,000 people located 25 miles southwest of Chicago. I have lived there my whole life. As we come over the giant gray concrete bridge that spans both the I &M canal and the Des Plaines River, the steeples of the five churches that dominate the skyline give the impression of a small, pious town. If you live there, however, you realize that for each Church in town there is also a bar. Lemont is a town of many dualities like that. Giant hills dominate the area, which is surrounded by flat Midwest farmland. The town had originally been built by hardworking men laboring in the quarries, but is now overpopulated with rich yuppies driving SUV's and BMW's. Soft businessmen in expensive suits now commission giant monoliths of the hard workers that had labored in the quarries while at the same time doing their best to keep chain business from getting business licenses. These actions combine to maintain their illusion of a small town. That illusion is shattered because the businessmen also tear down smaller, older homes and build giant modern castles in gated communities. I have lived there my whole life, and I both love and hate it.

I am pretty complicated like that, too.

∎∎

Turning into town, we begin to make our way up the hills to Ackmed's house. Chaos, similar what we had seen in the streets all morning, exists in town as well. The only difference is that now there are more zombies roaming around. A man wearing blue jeans and no shirt wanders in front of our car, but it's too late for me to swerve and avoid him. We slam into him, and No Shirt flips over us, cracking the windshield and landing in the street behind us. As we disappear around a corner, I see him in my rearview mirror. He is still moving, crawling after the car with his jaws snapping in eager anticipation of a meal.

"I guess we know that the zombies made it here." Kevin notices Ackmed's pained look. "I am sure your parents are fine, man. Your dad is a rocket scientist for God's sake. He is too smart to be bitten by a zombie."

Ackmed doesn't look reassured. He doesn't speak until we reach his house, a nice two story blue home with a black Audi parked in the driveway. A mailbox with a sign that reads, "The Sharma's" sits near the curb. Nothing seems amiss, except for the garden tools sitting in the yard and the abandoned lawnmower resting on the half cut lawn. Entering through the front door, we are greeted by Ackmed's parents. His father is a giant man with skin as dark as Mr. Humphrey's. He formally shakes each of our hands and tells us in his Indian accent how happy he is that we were safe. Ackmed's mother, a beautiful olive skinned woman from Saudi Arabia, gives us each a hug, thanking Allah that we are safe.

Sitting around their dining room table, we recount our story. Ackmed's father gasps when he hears of our morning adventure, frowning and shaking his head. When we finish, he tells us that Mrs. Sharma and he had been cleaning the yard when the zombies attacked. "When that man pushed Mrs. S down, I thought she was dead. Luckily, we were able to get into the house with no more than a few scratches."

The room comes to an instant silence. Ackmed's voice trembles. "Scratches?"

"Yes son, a few scratches, but nothing major. Don't worry, we are fine."

Kevin's face lights up like a light bulb. "That means that-"

Ackmed stands up and almost screams. "Let me see them."

"I don't see what the big deal is son," Mr. Sharma replies. "They are really minor wounds."

"Let me see them," Ackmed repeats, his tone rising to a fury.

Rising to his feet and pushing his sleeve back, Mr. Sharma reveals a red scratch about six inches long. It looks no worse than the scratches I used to get as a kid when I wrestled with my dog Butch. "Fine, fine. Are you happy now? It isn't a big deal. Your mother's scratch is half that size."

"Dad, this is very important. Did either of you bleed?"

"Bleed? Of course they bled, but only a little. We treated them with antiseptic and they stopped right away. Your mother is a doctor for God's sake. She knows what she is doing." Mr. Sharma sounds so sure of himself that I don't want to tell him the truth.

Ackmed begins to pace, tears streaming down his cheeks. His mother and father watch in apparent confusion as their only child walks back and forth across the room mumbling to himself. Mr. Sharma grunts, while Mrs. Sharma fights back tears. They must think that Ackmed has gone insane or something.

Ackmed fails to respond when they question him about what is wrong. He just walks back and forth slowly, arms in his pockets. He mumbles as he walks. "This can't be happening. This can't be happening."

But it is happening. We are living in the zombie apocalypse. Mr. Sharma looks to me and points at Ackmed. "What is wrong with him?"

Writer though I am, I cannot quite form the words to tell Mr. and Mrs. Sharma that according to our best guess, they are already dead. I begin to stumble my way through an explanation, but Ackmed interrupts me. Clenching his fists, he shouts, "Damn it Mom and Dad, you're going to turn into zombies. How could you let this happen? Have you never seen a horror movie? You run away from zombies. They are slow and dumb for Christ's sake. How could you let yourself get bitten?"

"Zombies? What is a zombie?" Mrs. Sharma pronounces it Zumbie. It is cute, but disheartening. They really are screwed.

Kevin calmly explains what a zombie apocalypse is, and how we were currently living in one. He then goes on to explain the ways of the undead, including how new zombies are formed. He pauses and looks at the floor. "I'm sorry. Based on everything we have read, you have only a few hours left before you get sick and then turn."

Ackmed throws his cup of tea at the wall. "How could you fucking do this to me?"

"Ackmed Sharma you will not talk to your mother that way." Mr. Sharma stands up and yells, pounding his fist on the table. He indicates Kevin and me with an outstretched finger. "Could you please excuse us for a moment?"

It is by far the most awkward situation I have ever been in, topping even that time in High School when I broke my own nose trying to undo Sally Crotchet's bra in a very uncomfortable place. (The back of her parents Volkswagen.) So I am glad when they leave the room. Kevin and I sit for several minutes, listening to muffled voices coming from the kitchen.

Eventually, the three emerge from the kitchen, arm in arm. All are crying, although Mr. and Mrs. Sharma look a bit pale already. They stand before us, a united family. Ackmed sniffles. "We are leaving."

I nod and say nothing. Kevin has less tact. "What about-"

"Don't worry about us. I am confident that this zombie legend is just a movie joke, and that it will not come true. However, Ackmed seems convinced that we are lost. If we are to turn into the undead, then I wouldn't want you boys to be here and put at risk. If I am right, and we are fine, we will call you in three days. If you don't hear from us by then, Ackmed is right, and we have turned. If this is the case, then I would charge you with watching over my son." Mr. Sharma sounds grave. Ackmed rolls his eyes through his tears, but remains silent.

I shake Mr. Sharma's hand. "I will keep him safe."

I sound unsure even to myself.

"If this zombie apocalypse nonsense is actually happening, then I would like for you boys to get somewhere safe as quickly as possible. Where will you go?"

"My house. It's just across town." I point vaguely in the direction of my house, even though Mr. Sharma has been there hundreds of times.

He doesn't seem to notice. "Good. Go now, and get to safety."

ONE

"What happened to them?" Sam is sitting forward in her seat, hands grasping her knees in anticipation.

I know that I am a good writer, but I am happy to learn that am I was a good story teller as well. Sam is literally on the edge of her seat. I have never had a beautiful woman focused completely on me before, and I have to fight to keep from telling her the end of the story right there. With the shirt she is wearing and the amount of cleavage I see as she leans forward, I would be hard pressed not to tell her my social security number and ATM PIN if she asked. Drawing on all my writer instincts, I force myself to ignore her cleavage. "I'll tell you in a second, it will all makes sense. The important thing to know is that we made it back to my house fine. For now, let's just say that Ackmed's parents never did call us."

It's always better to delay gratification, both in life and in storytelling.

"So they became zombies?" I must tell too good a story, because she really wants to know what happened. I feel a surge of annoyance, but try not to show it. This girl is paying attention to me after all. I can't alienate her.

"We weren't sure, because the phones were shut off soon after that. Something about the system becoming overloaded. No one called. But Mr. Sharma had told us not to come looking for him no matter what, so we didn't. It really seemed to eat at Ackmed. As time passed, he spent more and more time alone. He also began to enjoy killing the zombies a lot. He would get up early and shoot them, just for fun."

"You guys had guns at home?" Sam wrinkles her brow disapprovingly. She must be a Democrat.

"No, but we got some guns from my neighbors' houses, which we began to raid for supplies. None of them were home, so it wasn't really stealing. More like borrowing to survive." My voice has become quick, almost frantic, as I explain myself. For some reason, it is very important to me that Sam knows that we weren't stealing.

Desperation is not sexy, so I decide to return to storytelling. "Over the next couple of months, we adapted to the zombie apocalypse lifestyle pretty well. The power stayed on and operated normally. We later found out that the reason we didn't lose any service was an update made to the power stations in our area by Homeland Security. And here I was against the Patriot Act."

Sam giggles, putting her hand on my forearm the way girls do when you genuinely make them laugh. My face reddens and a warm tingling sensation fills my body. I like it. "Don't worry about it, I am against it too. But, in this case, I am glad it saved you."

We sit like that for a couple of seconds before she moves her hand away. I still feel the tingling sensation on my arm. Hoping that I can think of another joke funny enough to make her put her hand back on my arm, I continue. "We were pretty safe as long as we stayed in the house. We really only had to leave to go out and look for food. Kevin filmed some of our adventures using the camera that he accidently carried out with us when we fled from Big Choice. Kevin was a struggling film maker, and he viewed the zombie apocalypse as a giant documentary that could put his name on the map. I didn't think that it would get that much play though, because most of what we did was relatively boring."

"I didn't think that your videos were boring at all. They were well written and funny."

"Those are the videos that we posted online, and we didn't start that until we found Ryan."

Sam frowns in confusion. "Who's Ryan?"

"Ryan Hamstry was a menace to me in life. He was one of those kids that adults who don't really know him always seem to love. He went to state one year with the wrestling team, and was a halfway decent running back during the fall. His dimples and tanned muscular body attracted the attention of almost every girl in our class. He got A's and B's and charmed the teachers with quick answers. He always had a friend or two to say hello to when he walked through the halls."

I pause for breath and Sam smiles and nods. "But...."

"But all that disappeared when the teachers and other adults were gone. He mocked us all the time for playing Goldeneye 007."

"Oh my God, I loved that game. I played it all the time when I was in High School."

"We played it for hours too." This girl Sam is too good to be true. I have always dreamed about finding a woman that is as devoted to N64 shooters as I am. The fact that she is cute doesn't hurt either.

"It is probably the best game ever made," we say in unison and then laugh again. She touches my arm, this time not moving her hand away. It still feels warm and tingly, and I still like it. I again smell her perfume as she leans close. It somehow smells better and more feminine than before. The sweetness of it almost overpowers me, and I have to concentrate. "Girls we liked liked Ryan. He mocked us during our class presentations. And when he saw us in the hallway, he did things like knock the books we were carrying out of our hands."

"I knew a girl like that in High School. Her name was Meghan, and she tormented me for years because I read the Lord of the Rings." Sam blushes a bit and looks down at the table, but I don't think getting bullied was something that she should be ashamed of. Quite the contrary, when coupled with her revelations regarding Goldeneye, the idea of her being bullied makes me believe that Sam could be perfect.

Deciding to forgo proposing marriage for now, I go back to Ryan. "So you know the type? One day, as we were walking back to my house with some food, suddenly there was Ryan, right there in front of me. This is the apocalypse now, with no cops and no consequences. Imagine finding Meghan in such a position."

Sam smiles and rubs my arm. "Ryan was still muscular, although now he was not so athletic. He limped. The color of his skin reminded me of the gray on an Imperial Star Destroyer. Reveling at my newfound power over this evil creature, I led him into a neighbor's backyard. With Kevin filming it, I jumped on a trampoline and swung my axe through his neck, decapitating him. His severed head went up on a fence post. Kevin uploaded the video to YouTube, after adding in the words, 'The only good zombie is a dead zombie,' in the last frame over a picture of Ryan's impaled head."

"You guys made <u>Zombies on Trampolines</u>? I had no idea. I have seen the video, and quite frankly, always thought it was a bit sick." She pauses long enough to get me worried. "However now that I know who was impaled and why, I like it more."

Relief floods through me, and my voice becomes more confident. <u>Zombies on Trampolines</u> got 20,000 hits the first day, and began our internet fame. Once a week, we posted a video of a themed zombie kill. It was pretty easy to find one or two zombies at a time and lead them into some sort of trap, like the time we recreated the scene from <u>American Psycho</u> where Christian Bale drops a chainsaw onto the head of some girl."

"The third video, <u>Bowling for Zombies</u>, was homage to The <u>Big Lebowski</u>. It featured bowling style kills, and Ackmed jumping out of a moving car firing an automatic weapon at a zombie. <u>Bowling for Zombies</u> also launched our website."

"That's the first one of your videos that I saw. I love how you made the website a community as well as a movie site. I joined then and there." She is a member of the website too? This is fantastic.

"Well, we stole that idea from Rooster Teeth, so I can't take all the credit. As you know, the site became a huge success. Apparently, there were lots of people interested in seeing us kill the undead and chatting with us. I was even spending evenings chatting with a girl with the username Hester Prynne."

I stop, realizing that I had inadvertently mentioned Hester. The smile quickly fades from Sam's face and is momentarily replaced by a frown and an eye roll. Quickly reverting back to her smile, she grips my arm harder. These signs of jealousy fuel me to move past Hester as quickly as I can.

"By our sixth video, Cowboys and Zombies, we had sponsors, and a new appreciation for the difficulties of lassoing. In our seventh video, Ackmed killed a zombie while wearing a New Balance shirt and the money began to flow into our bank accounts. Two weeks later, when we finished shooting Harry Potter and the Zombies, I took a drink from a refreshing coke."

I decide that it is time for another joke. "Coke, the taste of the zombie killing generation."

Sam indicates the blue can on the table and smiles playfully. "I like Pepsi."

"Me too, but the great thing about sponsorship is that they paid me a lot of money to say that I liked Coke and I only had to drink one can of it. Then, I switched back to Pepsi."

Sam takes a drink of her Pepsi as I summarize how great our situation appeared that September. "Kevin was getting to make movies, Ackmed was getting to kill zombies, and I was talking to a girl online and writing internet shorts. We were all making money, and even if we didn't have anything to spend it on, eventually we would. As you know, the zombie outbreak had been mostly contained to the Midwest. Eventually, the Army would kill all the zombies, and we would have to go back to working at Big Choice and attending community college."

"If it was going so well for you, why did you stop making the theme kills? I was sad when they ended." I start to feel a bit annoyed because Sam has again interrupted me. That feeling fades as she flips her brown hair over her ear again. I notice that it looks really soft.

Sam fills the silence. "Not that I didn't enjoy the other movies of course."

All is forgiven. "Well we decided to change our website's direction the day we went to Mr. Chimelski's house."

A man and a woman stumble towards me. The man is closer. As he limps up to me, he sniffs the air and lets out a groan. He has on jean shorts and a dirty black t-shirt that reads, "2005 world champion Chicago White Sox," in big white letters. Great, a fucking Sox fan. The woman, who is directly behind him, has on a tight jean skirt, one cheap purple stiletto heel, and a shirt two sizes too small that has the word, "Princess," in silver glittery letters. Just your typical White Sox couple, out on a morning stroll from the trailer park.

As Sox Fan comes within reaching distance, he stiffens and moans something incomprehensible. I swing my axe like a baseball player lunging for a high fastball. The sharp silver head of the axe hits Sox Fan in the neck, slicing through flesh, bone, and muscle. Blood the color of an eggplant flows from shattered jugular veins. Grunting with effort, I put my entire body into the swing, and the axe continues its journey through sinewy muscle and fat. Sox's head pops off and lands face down in a puddle, splashing bloody water onto my shoes. Home run.

That blow, while it looked really cool, is a mistake and I know it. It takes a lot of effort to severe someone's head, and the force of the blow spins me completely around. I drop my axe and fall to one knee. Princess moans, and I know that she is right behind me. Glancing over my shoulder, I see her tiny, outstretched arm reaching for me. On her bicep, a tattoo of a heart with the letters DW in the center of it stands bright red against her skin. Just as her arm is about to reach me, I frantically kick my leg out. It is a desperate, clumsy move, but I manage somehow to connect with Princess's stomach. The blow pushes her back a foot or two and gives me the moment I need to scramble to my feet. I bring the axe up just in time to deflect her next attack. As Princess launches a third attack, I swing the axe over my head and bury it into her skull. She grunts again and falls to the ground with a thud. I stand there watching her body, my arms shaking a little bit. That was close, as close as it has ever been.

"I thought I was going to have to save your ass man, and on camera too."

I turn and see Kevin and Ackmed staring at me. Ackmed has drawn his katana, and its silver light glistens in the sunlight. Kevin has a small flip video camera aimed at me. He grins at me and says, "Got it. It will look great!"

Their enthusiasm boosts me, and I forget how close the arm with the DW tattoo was to me and how desperate my kick was. This is my world. I am in control. I am a bad ass. "It looks like they are all gone. Too bad. I had something special planned for Charlene here."

I pat my knife, an 8 inch serrated blade that I found four days ago in the home of my neighbor, a kind man from South Carolina that Ackmed shot early one morning with a triumphant victory whoop that woke Kevin and I. We named the knife Charlene after the rifle from Full Metal Jacket.

"You have been saying that for days now, and that knife hasn't been used for anything but opening a can of corn." Ackmed holds up his clean sword. In a terrible Australian accent, he says, "You call that a knife? Now this is a knife."

Kevin folds the camera and puts it back into his pocket. "Let's get moving to Mr. Chimelski's house. I want to go back and upload this soon."

"Yeah, I do have my fans to worry about."

We walk the remaining block from my house in silence. This is the farthest that any of us has been in the last three months, and we are not quite sure what we will find. We don't see anyone else, although there are some mutilated bodies in various states of decomposition scattered about on the street and in the yards near us. Flies buzz, and there are more black crows than I remember.

Our destination is a red brick two story house with an evergreen tree in the front yard. The grass is months overgrown, which makes sense, because I haven't mowed it recently. On the sidewalk in front of the house someone, Mr. Chimelski probably, scratched "Ed and Jean- 1981" into the cement when it was wet. A body sits on the lawn, bloated with death, the flesh almost completely picked away by birds. Flies buzz around the body, finishing what flesh birds left. I can tell that it is Mr. Chimelski, the old man whose lawn I used to mow, because of the light mesh fedora that lays near the body. He always wore that hat when he went outside.

I point at the mound of flesh and bone. "That's him,"

Kevin averts his eyes. "Shit man. I'm sorry for your loss. That sucks."

It does suck. Mr. Chimelski had been a nice man. I had been mowing his grass since I was 14, when the then 80 year old widower had his first heart attack. We were not friends or anything, and he certainly wasn't a mentor. He was just a nice man whose lawn I mowed for 15 dollars a week. Sometimes he would tell dirty jokes that used to make me flush with the embarrassment of a teenager realizing that an old man knew all about sex. I didn't really know anything about him, just that he missed his wife, who had died the year before I started mowing his grass. It still sucked that he was dead. He never had a chance. I felt a rush of sadness wash over me.

On the heels of that rush was a wave of guilty relief. Mr. Chimelski's death may even save our lives. Had he lived, we would have had to take him back to my house. An old man with health problems is not something that we needed slowing us down.

"Sad." Ackmed's voice is flat, without a hint of emotion. He begins to walk toward the door. "Let's get inside and get back."

Kevin takes out his camera again. "Wait a second. Here comes Andy."

I turn and see a figure about 15 feet away. He must have approached us quietly, like a ninja. Hugely fat, the giant zombie ninja looks to be in his mid 20's, just like us. It is in fact, Andy Sartine. At 6 foot 4 and 350 pounds, Andy was an all state offensive tackle in high school. When he graduated, he got a full ride to the University of Illinois to play football. There was even talk of his going pro someday. Unfortunately Andy was dumb as a rock, and failed out of school after just a semester. So instead of playing in the NFL, Andy came back home to Lemont and worked as a janitor at the local grade school. Andy had blue eyes that, if they didn't have that divine spark of intelligence, at least possessed a dull kindness. Kind of like a big, dumb, friendly dog. I had liked Andy in high school.

Now, he approached me wearing his old high school gym shirt and a pair of shorts. There was dried blood in his short dark hair and on his face. His glasses had a crack in the lens, but he didn't seem to notice. His eyes don't have kindness behind them now. They look, for lack of a better description, dead. There is nothing behind them, like the eyes of a character in CG animation. Lifelike, but not quite real.

Kevin begins to raise his camera, but I tell him not to film this one. "We know Andy."

"Well, we knew Ryan, too, but that didn't stop you from uploading that shit to YouTube." Ackmed's face is concerned, and I can tell he thinks that I am going soft. Between this, and the near miss I had with Princess, I can't say I blame him much.

"Ryan was a douche bag. That fucker terrorized us since we were in the 4th grade. We like Andy." Andy, who is about 5 feet away from me, groans as if he hears his name.

"We liked him." Andy is four feet away now. There are streaks of yellow crumbs on his shirt from his last meal, which looks to have been Cheetos.

I have no answer for Ackmed, but with Andy this close I don't want to waste time thinking of a witty response or rational justification for what I am about to do. Pulling out an old pistol, I ignore Ackmed and Kevin's protesting shouts and shoot Andy in the face. The gunshot is loud, piercing the morning quiet. Andy falls to the ground without even a groan. Nice, quick, and as dignified as it gets these days.

"What the fuck was that?" Ackmed screams, searching the block for anyone approaching. "Not only was that a waste of bullets, but now we are going to be fucked. They are going to come in from all directions, you fucking dumbass."

"Andy was our friend, kind of. He was always nice to us. He didn't deserve to have his head smashed in, or have his death broadcast for the world's amusement."

"That's what we do now. We amuse people. Or at least Kevin and I do."

Before I can answer, Kevin interrupts, "Let's get inside Mr. Chimelski's house before they show up. Ackmed, go upstairs. I'll clear the middle floor while Malcolm takes the basement. We will meet up down there and stay out of sight."

Ackmed pushes past me, shoving me so hard that I stumble and fall down next to Andy's body, which already has flies buzzing around it. I lay on the concrete in disbelief. Ackmed, who did nothing in response to 18 years of harassment by people who didn't like the idea of anyone in Lemont that wasn't white, had just shoved me to the ground.

Ackmed doesn't look back as he trots up to Mr. Chimelski's house. An errant fly buzzes into my open mouth and gets stuck in my throat. I cough, trying to get the fly out, but it does no good. I begin to gag, and without warning, vomit. I open my eyes when I am done and find myself face to face with Andy's body. There is a hole in his forehead from where I shot him. Blood and brain matter surround the hole. Andy's eyes are still open, blue and lifeless. He smells sickly sweet, like decaying flesh. I gag again, and vomit a second time.

Kevin leans down and pats me on the shoulder. "Ackmed is shutting down emotionally man. It's how he is dealing. He's been getting farther away. Don't worry about it; he will be ok soon. Now get up before we have company."

Standing up, I find that I am shaking and weak. My stomach, chest, and neck hurt from the muscles contracting, and I am breathing quickly. For a second, my vision is cloudy. I stumble after Kevin, almost tripping over Mr. Chimelski's body and disturbing the flies that still buzz around him. I fight the urge to vomit again.

This is the zombie apocalypse, and I am a badass.

TWO

I hate clearing houses. They are cramped and there is not always an escape route. It is easy to get boxed in. On the street, in the open, I am a bad ass. On the street, in front of the camera, I am not a 25 year old junior college student who still lives with his parents. On the street, I am a zombie killing machine. I have testicles the size of bowling balls. I have no fear and can do anything. All of the things we did on YouTube, all of the things that we had become famous for- or at least internet famous for- in the last few months, all of it was controlled.

In the case of the daily kills, like the one we had just filmed, we were always near a safe house. We could run inside, shut the door, and hide out if more zombies came. Someone was always standing by to help. Kevin, or more likely Ackmed, was always there with a sword or an axe or even a gun. The zombies we killed were usually alone or in pairs. There was almost no danger.

The theme kills were the same. We lured the zombies to us, killing them off except for the ones we wanted for our traps. Honestly, those were kind of like playing a video game. We were never so cool or alive than we were when we filmed the theme kills.

But now there are no cameras rolling. Now I am walking into Mr. Chimelski's house with my axe held high, looking for zombies. Kevin heads toward the front room to begin his search of the middle floor. Upstairs, I hear Ackmed walking around, slowly and methodically searching each room. I am alone in front of a terrifying door that leads to the basement. The door had never looked ominous before. It was always just a plain wooden door with a calendar that had a picture of an American flag on it. It had just been the door to the basement, an entry or exit, something to go through when I carried something heavy upstairs or downstairs for Mr. Chimelski. Now, it could be the gateway to hell. The basement could have zombies in it. Another person might have known about Mr. Chimelski's wonderful freezer, stocked full of frozen meats. That person might have come here and been bitten, or had a member of their party bitten, and then turn on them. That basement could be full of zombies. That door could be the last doorway I would ever go through. My stomach feels like it is about to crawl up through my throat again. My legs are tense, and I am sweating. At this point, my balls are the size of BB's, not bowling balls.

I imagine four or five recently deceased ghouls wandering about downstairs, eager for their first kill. Ackmed says that I think about shit too much. As a writer, I do have an active imagination, which serves me well most of the time. However, at times like this, I need to remember Ackmed's advice and not think too much.

I open the wooden door slowly, half expecting something to jump at me. Nothing happens, and I figure that Ackmed must be right. After all, fortune favors the brave, and it might just still be the door to the basement. Nothing much happens right away. It is totally dark downstairs, and through the open door I can see the first two or three steps leading downstairs and the familiar wooden had rail on the right. There is a light switch next to the door, and I am not sure whether or not to turn it on. It might alert the zombies, if there are any. Then again, the thought of entering that basement in total blackness and having to find, fight, and subdue a horde of undead in the dark makes my legs literally begin to buckle, so I flick the light switch on.

The dark, gaping maw goes away, and is replaced with the familiar sights of the basement. The steps are painted gray and are the kind of slick steps that you never much pay attention to until you fall down them once or twice. There is an American Flag on the wall and various tools around the landing. Nothing moves in front of me, so I gingerly make my way down the stairs. They creak as I step on them. I forgot that they did that. Still, nothing moves in front of me. I enter the basement itself, which is unfinished concrete. Once I am down the stairs, the basement is pretty much one big room, except for the area directly behind me, which is blocked by the staircase. This makes it easy to see that there is nothing down in the basement except Mr. Chimelski's old rusted tools and about 10 large remote control planes that he built and flew. I search behind the staircase, and there is also nothing, except the wonderful untouched white freezer. I open the freezer, and it is all there. Steaks to last us at least a month or two, chicken breasts, a whole turkey, and even a frozen apple pie. Jackpot.

Despite my becoming a pussy, I can apparently still find food.

I sit down in a folding chair that is in the basement. I feel guilty. I have, it seems, failed yet again. Up until this time, I had accepted that I was a failure in real life. If my parents didn't remind me enough, most of the angry customers in Big Choice vented their frustrations by calling me a loser of some kind. This world was different. In this world, the one with zombies, I was good at something. I could write funny skits and fight off evil monsters. Now, though, I didn't think that I could do that anymore.

Andy was the first person that I had known in life who became a zombie. There was Ryan, of course, but I hated Ryan. I had killed him in my mind hundreds of times over the years. Ryan was no big deal.

Andy, however, was different. He was a real person. He was a nice guy. And that was a problem.

Because, if Andy was a real person, and a nice guy, then so was everyone else that we had killed.

For the last couple of months, the three of us had done things. Things that now seemed terrible to me. We had turned this zombie apocalypse into a game. I look at the gray concrete ground, fighting back tears as I realize that I can't play that game anymore. I couldn't make it in the first world that I had been in, and now I can't make it in this one either.

I am a pussy.

The stairs creak again, and Ackmed comes down. We stare at each other, saying nothing. I want to yell. I want to scream to him, "What happened to you man?" I want to ask him how he could ever hit me. I want to ask him if he remembers when Kevin and I were his only friends, if he remembers when Ryan Hamstry mercilessly teased him, and when Kevin and I stood up for him. I want to tell him that I am sorry that his parents are dead. I want to tell him that I am his family, that he is my brother. I want to tell him that we can only survive if we work together. I want to say all of this, and more, but the words do not form.

So instead of saying all that, we just sit and stare at each other, breathing in the musty basement air.

"You hit me." The voice is that of a child, whiney and shocked. The voice is my own, though I don't know exactly how the words I was thinking became that pathetic sentence. God damn it, I am a bad ass.

Ackmed doesn't answer, so remembering that I am a bad ass, I stand to my full height. "I said you hit me. What the fuck man?" To my relief, my voice is less shaky this time, and sounds more angry than scared.

Ackmed continues to stare at me.

The stairs creak again, and Kevin appears. He looks around the room, perhaps searching for something neutral to say. "The house is clear."

No one responds to this obvious statement. If the house was not clear, we would not be standing here. We would be fighting zombies. Or dead.

Kevin seems unnerved by the silence, and begins talking quickly, asking questions but not pausing long enough to receive an answer. "Is the food here? Good. Yeah man, they are coming now outside. There are probably 40 or 50 of them in the street already, but I don't think any of them saw us."

Eventually, he has to pause to take a breath, and Ackmed stands up, still staring at me. He crosses the room and approaches me quickly. I tense, and prepare myself for a fight. If he decides to hit me, he will probably use his right hand to hit me, because he is right handed. I can twist to my left punch him in the ribs. Ackmed stops about 3 feet from me. He is still staring at me, but suddenly, he looks down as if ashamed, and says, "I'm sorry that I hit you, Malcolm."

"Look, man, we need to talk. We need to figure out what to do."

"Well, we have plenty of time. They aren't going to go away for at least 3 or 4 hours." Kevin, although looking relieved that Ackmed and I are not going to begin beating each other, is still talking too fast and stating the obvious.

Ackmed ignores Kevin. "Yeah you are right."

"Look, I don't like this. I don't want to keep making theme kills." Now it is my turn to look at the ground in shame.

Now, it's out there. I am officially a real pussy.

Kevin and Ackmed look at me like I just suggested we have a threesome together. They both begin talking at once, Kevin discussing how he is a filmmaker now, and Ackmed angrily talking about how much money we will lose. Eventually, they are done, or at least need to pause for a breath, and I explain to them my newfound theory of zombies as people. Now, they stare at me as if I just suggested that I want to be the finger cuffs in the middle of that threesome I suggested earlier.

"So, let me get this straight, you're suggesting that we stop killing zombies, right here in the middle of the zombie apocalypse?" Ackmed scrunches up his face like he is trying to puzzle out a really difficult math equation.

"No, I am not suggesting that at all. Look, if we have to kill some zombies when we get out of here, so be it. If we have to kill some to survive, then let's do it. But we are luring zombies in for sport. For some video on the internet that a kid can watch. Think about it man, we are killing people for that. It's not cool."

"But they are dead already. We aren't killing anyone. That's the definition of a zombie. The walking dead. The undead. I mean, their name even has the word dead in it." Ackmed laughs, as if making a joke will fix me.

"Ackmed, those people were someone to somebody. If they are dead, then fine, we are not killing them. But, they are still bodies, even if they are animated. And we should treat them with some kind of respect, at least for their families, if not for the people they used to be."

"Respect? Treat them with respect? Dude, you have said it yourself, most people are assholes. How many people treated us with respect before this? How many of the people they used to be would yell at us for not being able to fix their computer, or take a return? Fuck them, and fuck their families too."

I don't want to use it, but I do. "Ackmed, what if we filmed us killing your parents and put it up on the internet?"

He doesn't hit me with his right hand, like I thought he would. He screams and charges me, knocking me onto the cold concrete floor. Pinning me to the ground, he hits me in the face a couple of times before Kevin pulls him off of me. I knew I shouldn't have used it.

I sit up. My lip is bleeding and my back hurts. I fight to catch my breath. I was not expecting that response from Ackmed. We haven't really talked about his parent's death too much, but I was kind of hoping that he would recognize my point of view in a kind of "Hallmark" moment. He would realize the full extent of his grief, maybe even cry a little, and agree with me. Instead, he only recognized the extent of his anger; and he vented that anger onto my face.

Who the fuck did he think he was, anyway? I had been hit enough in High School, and I didn't want to ever be picked on again. He was picking on me. Hitting me twice in the span of about 10 minutes, that is picking on me. My friend indeed. I feel powerful as I stand up. Reaching back, I hit Ackmed with a massive shoryken punch to his jaw. It hurts my hand, but it hurts his face more. He can't even block the punch, because Kevin is still holding him back from attacking me. The blow knocks both of them to the ground. Kevin rolls to his right, and starts to back up as I kick Ackmed once in the stomach. "I am sick of you hitting me, motherfucker, and it's going to stop right now. You didn't answer my question, asshole, but I am guessing that you wouldn't like it very much if I took your parents death and put it up on the internet with a funny caption like "Shitty parents that raise stupid child become zombies.""

Ackmed regains his breath just enough to tell me to go fuck myself, which is not a witty retort. I have the upper hand now, and it feels just great. Orgasmic even. I am finally standing up for myself. Years of being picked on by various bullies bleed off of me as I kick Ackmed in the stomach again. I can do anything I want to Ackmed right now. I am in control. I am 8 feet tall, my dick is a foot long in the snow, and I have brass nuts the size of bowling balls. I am a badass.

On my left, I hear the distinct click of a gun being cocked, and Kevin's voice, no longer talking too fast but still stating the obvious. "Stop it or I am going to shoot you."

Three

Kevin is holding the gun at my right eye. That gaping black hole is all I can see in the entire world.

"Look, we need to all relax for a bit. So everybody calm the fuck down."

I step back, away from Ackmed. Even though he didn't ask, I raise my hands. "Does that include not pointing the gun at me anymore?"

Kevin lowers the gun. He still has it out, but it isn't pointed at me anymore. "It's always hardest to see your own problems."

Moving to opposite corners of the room, Ackmed and I continue to stare at each other. My face still hurts, and all of the muscles in my body are sore. Ackmed pulls himself into a sitting position and throws up. He collapses onto his back when he is done, holding he holds his stomach with both hands and moaning. He sounds a bit like a zombie. Kevin continues to chatter on about mindless things, but too softly for me to hear.

After a while, Kevin begins to speak. He tells us in a professorially voice that we all have issues to resolve with each other. Two years earlier, Kevin went out on exactly two dates with a therapist. She told him one night over a steak dinner that the important thing to resolving conflicts is being able to see the other person's side of a problem. Over a dessert of cheesecake, she then told Kevin to think using the other person's emotions instead of your own opinions to find a resolution. After that, she refused to pay for the check and told Kevin she preferred not to let him up to her apartment for a nightcap. Bitch.

Ever since that time, however, Kevin has fancied himself an amateur psychologist. He was always trying to see another side to things, a trait that drove Ackmed and I crazy. Someone couldn't just be an asshole anymore; they had to have a reason for it. Despite our best efforts,

Kevin enrolled in several psychology courses. He began to use terminology like repressing rage and feelings of inadequacy when discussing our asshole customers like Mr. Humphrey. I think had this whole zombie thing not happened, he would have eventually ditched film for therapy.

Warning us that no more violence would be tolerated, he began to tell us our issues. Ackmed was angry at his parent's untimely deaths, and I have major issues with authority and control. "As for me, I am just not that great at dealing with issues head on. Usually, I just talk about something else, mostly the obvious."

Ackmed and I begin to laugh. Kevin puts the gun down on the ground. Looking at Ackmed, he says, "I am sorry your parents died. But….it's not your fault."

"Mork from Ork is right, Ackmed," I chime in, smiling. "It's not your fault."

"Good Will Hunting, great movie man. How do you like them apples?" Ackmed mimics planting a fake paper against fake glass.

"Applesauce, bitch." That one came from Jay and Silent Bob Strike Back. Classic.

Raising his voice a bit like a teacher trying to get an unruly class's attention, Kevin tells us, "Ok nice, but not now. Now is not the time for jokes man, or bad movie quotes."

"First of all, Jay and Silent Bob is a good movie. Second of all, Good Will Hunting won an Academy award and launched the careers of two of Hollywood's most beloved leading men,"

"I said knock it the fuck off man," Kevin's yells, now sounding like a teacher rapidly losing control of his class. He looks at the gun; he doesn't pick it up, he just looks at it like a construction worker choosing a tool for a particular project. Ackmed and I stop laughing, and the room is plunged into another silence.

I hate long silences and serious conversations, but sometimes I guess they have to occur. I study the ceiling for a while. It is unfinished, and there are fifteen 2X4's running lengthwise across it. That serious math equation solved, I endure the silence until it becomes too much. I give Ackmed my most concerned face. "I am sorry about your parents too, man. There was nothing you or any of us could do."

That seems good enough to please Kevin, who clasps his hands together and sits forward. "Good, man. Is there anything you would like to say to Malcolm, Ackmed?"

"I know you are sorry, and I appreciate it." Ackmed's voice is shaky, and Kevin and I pretend not to notice the two wet lines running down his face. "It just….sucks so much, you know?"

"I do know man," says Kevin, his voice cracking a bit. "Remember, I've been there."

Kevin's parents had been killed in a car accident during our senior year of high school, which is roughly around the time he moved in with me. It is also why he was still living in our basement when the zombies came six years later.

There is another long, drawn out silence. Seizing on the chance to lighten the mood, I make an angry face. "Well, my parents are still alive, and fuck both of you for leaving me out of the conversation." We all laugh, and Ackmed helpfully tells me that my parents, who were vacationing in Hawaii when the uprising in the Midwest started, could have died in a surfing accident or been eaten by a shark.

"Thanks man, that makes me feel better."

"I am sorry that I hit you. And then hit you again," Ackmed suddenly says before we can lapse into silence again.

"It's cool man, I did kick you a couple of times." I get up and put my hand out to Ackmed, an olive branch, but he stands up and hugs me. He tells me that Kevin and I are the only family he has left. Kevin gets up and hugs us both, and says, "Brothers don't shake hands, brothers got to hug."

We sit down, closer together now. Great, one crisis averted. We are joking around again, discussing the top 10 best orphan movies. We move from Peter Pan to Hook to Oliver Twist (ok technically Oliver Twist isn't a movie, but I do have an English background- I am 10 credits short of graduating from College of Dupage with an Associate's degree in English.) Kevin glances at his watch and tells us that an hour has passed since I shot Andy. We still have a little while before most of the zombies get bored looking for us and begin to search for different food.

The zombies that we are dealing with have some kind of ADD or something; after hearing a noise, they flock to the area, but after a time, usually four or five hours, they begin to disperse. I guess they figure that there will be easier prey elsewhere or something. We know if one sees you, that zombie will stay longer than the rest, but the undead have no way of communicating that there is actual food in the area, so the other zombies usually search elsewhere. Thus, our goal is to hang out in the basement as long as possible before leaving for home.

This leaves us plenty of time to discuss the future of our company and the way that we are handling the zombie apocalypse. For a while, we ignore the problem. It is just like it used to be, just like it always has been. We have a long discussion about what ever could have possessed George Lucas to have Greedo shoot first. After much debate, we decide that it is an early symptom of the dementia that would eventually manifest itself fully during the production of the Phantom Menace. We rework our list of the top 10 video games of all time, with Goldeneye 007 for the Nintendo 64 still coming in first place, followed closely by *The Elder Scrolls: Oblivion*. Rooster Teeth's Red VS. Blue still comes in first for best web series, and Chasing Amy still is the best Kevin Smith movie. (Sorry Cop Out.) Eventually our movie quotes and lists run out, and another long silence occurs. I don't want to break this one, because I know what everyone is thinking about.

Eventually, Kevin's voice pierces the silence. "So, what do we do now?"

Ackmed's answer is simple. "We survive."

An elegant solution that should solve the problem until the government can bail us out. Since we weren't IAG or too big to fail, that could be quite a while.

"That's easy for you to say, Ackmed. You just want to kill zombies. You can do that and survive." Kevin tells us that he wants to keep making movies. He is a director now, and to him, directing our little movies makes him feel as if he had, "broken the bonds that kept him shackled to a boring life before."

"Obviously, you're not a writer, too. That was pathetic."

"No, that's you Malcolm. You're the writer. Wouldn't you miss writing themed kill skits? I mean in the that last one, when the fake Harry Potter says the line about the zombie who didn't live, that was really clever. I know that you have been having fun writing these, don't even try to deny it."

I have to admit, it was true. I enjoyed writing cheesy dialogue and one liners. I was even writing a fiction book about a loser in his mid 20's who is thrust into the zombie apocalypse. The main character thrives in this environment. I don't know if anything will ever come of it. I am three chapters in, and am still not sure who would want to read a book about a loser and some zombies.

"So. I want to make movies, Ackmed wants to survive and kill zombies, and Malcolm wants to write. "

"I want more than just to kill zombies."

Ackmed sounds like I do when my parents tell me all I want to do is live in their basement and play video games my whole life. Offended, and a little hurt.

Kevin pulls a good line out of his bag of therapy tricks. "Ok, Ackmed, what do you want to do?"

"I want to do something that benefits other people, not just makes them laugh. I want to do something for the greater good."

I am so taken aback by this idea that I nearly forget to say, "The greater good." Movie quotes, even in a time of great crisis, must always be observed. Besides, Hot Fuzz is a great flick.

As a fellow redhead, I really like Simon Pegg. Like him, I am creative. I may not be as funny, as talented, or as British, but I am almost as creative. And being creative means that you get to things like sit straight up, point at the sky, and shout something incredibly original. "Aha. I've got it."

The others look at me like I just had a seizure. "I have an idea. It will work."

Kevin shakes his head and gives me an exasperated half smile."Great. I can't wait to hear how I can direct, you can write, and Ackmed can help people, all without killing zombies just for the pure fun of it."

Four

I never get sick of watching myself on the internet. On the flat panel monitor, I hold up a fake microphone and give the camera a fake newscaster smile.

"Now, I know that it can be terrifying to live in the zombie apocalypse, but I am here to tell you that it's not that bad." I am wearing a suit. It is way too big for me, as it is not mine. Thank God for suspenders.

"Zombies may look like people, but we have several advantages over them. We are stronger and faster. Our most precious asset, however, is our brain. The average zombie has the intelligence of a rock, while the average American is slightly smarter than that." I smile reassuringly at the camera. You can see some sweat on my forehead, but the internet should understand. I am in a suit in my backyard in the Midwest, and it is mid September.

"Welcome to *This Old Zombie*, the show that makes zombie killing easy."

The credits begin to roll, and videos of us killing zombies fill the screen. The song Kick Some Ass by Stroke 9 plays. Ackmed slices off a zombies head and blood gushes out. The camera freezes on an awesome shot of him holding up a dripping red sword and the words, "Ackmed Sharma," appear under him. The same introduction occurs for all three of us. It is a classic 80's montage opening. And it is awesome. The screen fades to black, and as the music quiets down, the words, "Hosted by Malcolm Tushton" fill the screen. I am famous.

I appear in the suit again, sweatier this time. I wish that there was a way to Photoshop the sweat out, but none of us know how Photoshop works. "Before we begin, let me introduce you to our zombie killing team. Ackmed Sharma has been killing zombies for three months. His weapon of choice is a sword, which we will get back to in a moment. Ackmed, how are you doing today?"

"I'm good Malcolm. It is a beautiful late September day, and I am ready to show the audience how to slay some fiends." Ackmed smiles. It's easy for him to say that it is a beautiful day out today. He is wearing shorts and a t-shirt.

"Great. Hold that thought. Before we get back to Ackmed, I would like to introduce the audience to the man behind the camera. Ladies and gentlemen, say hello to our director, camera man, and editor Kevin Jones."

Another camera, operated by Ackmed, focuses in on Kevin. He looks very directorial, half his face peeking out from behind the camera as he waves. He even has a beard.

"Ok, since this is our first show, we are going to cover the most basic zombie lesson possible: how to kill a zombie. The thought of eradicating an undead body from the earth is a little daunting, but in actuality, it can be easier than killing a live human. Ackmed, why don't you tell us a little about that."

"Well, as Malcolm says, in many ways killing a zombie is much easier than killing a person. They are slow and dumb, and don't understand the concept of danger at all. That said, these guys are impervious to gunshots, stab wounds, arrows, and anything else that human beings can throw at them." Ackmed pauses dramatically. "Unless you hit them in the head."

"So the head is really the Achilles heel of the zombies?"

"That's right, Malcolm. The head is the foot, in this case. Do anything you want to their head. Slice it off, shoot it, stab it, or put an arrow through the brain. Whatever tickles your fancy. It's like we always say, go for the head, and he will be dead."

All three of us say this last sentence, which we have decided is going to be our tagline.

"Today, Ackmed is going to show us how to kill a zombie, with the help of our friend Zach here." The camera shows a zombie that we lured into my backyard ambling up to us. He is wearing a striped sweater, which makes him kind of look like a decrepit Where's Waldo. In deference to our newfound respect of him, Zach's face is blurred out. The shot reminds me of a classier version of cops.

"Now it is important to remember that these videos are made by professionals, and that you should only attempt to perform these maneuvers if your immediate safety is threatened. In other words, don't be the guy who dies doing something he saw on the internet."

Ackmed waits as the zombie approaches, and I continue. "Now Ackmed is letting the zombie come to him, which is also very important. Choose your own battleground, where you are comfortable fighting. The zombie won't care where you go, so pick a place that you like."

When the zombie is five feet away, Ackmed draws his katana. Its silvery blade glistens in the sunlight. "Ackmed is drawing his Katana, so it looks like he is planning on a straight decapitation kill here." I sound like Alton Brown describing the use of an ingredient on Iron Chef.

"Remember before when we told you that zombies are dumb? Well this is perfect proof of that." Ackmed slashes the sword and flicks the zombie off. "Come here you big dumb zombie. Come get your head chopped off by this big sword, you idiot."

Zach, oblivious to the shouting, continues to limp forward at a steady pace. As he gets closer to Ackmed, I continue to speak in my Alton Brown voice. "Now the thing to remember about decapitation kills is that it requires several different things. You need a lot of strength to chop a head off with a weapon like a sword, so ladies may want to think of using a different technique. It also takes a lot of time, so use this move only when you are sure there isn't another ghoul lurking behind you."

Ackmed chops off Zach's head off, and it rolls behind him. Zach's body falls to the ground. Ackmed says, "Zach zero, humanity one."

"Easy as pie, Ackmed. Any last tips you might have for our viewers at home?"

"Get a good wide stance, and use all of your strength. Oh, and, clean your blade off after your kills. It prevents rust." He wipes the blade off on the grass and smiles.

"You have been watching *This Old Zombie*. Tune in next week when we show you how to pick the perfect weapon. Stay safe, and if all else fails, remember to go for the head, and he will be dead."

Credits roll as Louie Armstrong sings "What a Wonderful World."

That first video got more hits than every Themed Zombie Kill combined. The *Today Show* ran a clip of it. Even though the outbreak was contained to the Midwest, it seemed like every American wanted to log on to our website and see how to kill a zombie. I guess people were afraid of a widespread outbreak. Perhaps they wanted to watch us kill zombies, but the idea of us mutilating corpses for fun was too much. Packaged as a how to video, the clips could allow them to indulge their disgusting sides while still maintaining a moral superiority. People are sick.

This Old Zombie was born.

■■■

Five

Sam fixes me with a dazzling smile that makes me almost jump with excitement. "I liked *This Old Zombie*. It made me feel safer, in case an attack happened near here. It was also pretty funny. "

"That's what we were going for. We wanted people to enjoy feeling safe, and they did. Six weeks into production, we had already gotten over 100,000 members on our website. We were just beginning to get phone calls from more sponsors. Bass Pro Shops wanted us to only use equipment from their store."

"So, did you? I never saw any of that on the website."

"The closest Bass Pro Shop was too far to risk it. It's a shame; they offered us so much money. Also, we were comfortable with the weapons that we had taken. Using new ones would feel wrong, and I didn't want to sell out."

Sam's brown eyes glint behind her blocky school teacher glasses. "You mean like drinking Coke?"

"Ok, well I didn't want to sell out completely."

"So what was it like? I mean the everyday life? Was it hard to survive? Were you busy setting up episodes?"

"No, it was really easy. We were still eating the food we had taken from Mr. Chimelski's freezer. We only shot *This Old Zombie* one day a week. Since most of the tasks we depicted were simple, it only took a few hours to write the script and less than a day to shoot each episode. As fucked up as it sounds, I don't think that I have ever been happier than September of last year. Each day, I would sleep until about 11. Generally, I would then get up and work on my book for a couple of hours before playing XBOX 360. I became so good at Modern Warfare 2, I eventually became a Colonel."

"I'm a General, but I can show you some tricks to up your score if you want. But weren't you lonely?" Sam leans forward to show me more cleavage. We both pretend that she hadn't just mentioned our meeting again. I think that I have just gotten a second date with her.

"I wasn't lonely at all. I guess I kind of missed my parents a bit, but from the emails we exchanged, they were happy. The government was paying for them to stay in Hawaii. I had my two best friends with me, and I could do whatever I wanted. There were no customers yelling at me, and no societal pressure to go out and make something of myself. I could read, write, or just watch TV. I found myself dreading the inevitable government rescue. "

"Did you guys watch it on TV? I paid attention for a little bit, but after they put up that wall around the Midwest, the progress seemed kind of slow and boring."

"Every night. I would have been ok watching once a week or so, but Ackmed has thing for newswomen. He would flip between MSNBC and CNN until he found a girl he liked. Sometimes, we would even watch Fox News. The channel really didn't matter because everyone showed the same thing- a map of the Midwest with a red circle around it representing the infection zone and a colored graphic representing our army. Each channel had a different color graphic- on CNN it was green, on Fox it was Red, and on MSNBC it was blue. As there was nothing else on the map, it was pretty easy for us to follow what was happening. The graphic and the Army were slowly advancing toward Chicago. Every day, without fail, it moved a bit closer to us."

As I am talking, I notice that Sam keeps looking around the room. She sits sat back in her chair, moving her warm hand away and making me lose sight of her cleavage. She must be getting bored of listening to stories about us watching TV.

"So what about Hester? Were you still talking to her?" Sam uses that nonchalant tone people do when they desperately want to know the answer to a question, but want you to think that they aren't interested. This girl must be totally into me.

"We still talked, but I hadn't updated my facebook status or anything yet. Let's just say I hoped that she wasn't a guy in real life, or I was going to need a therapist."

She pretends to laugh, but I can tell that it is the kind of laugh that a woman gives a man when she doesn't think that he is particularly funny. Looking around the room again, she sips her Pepsi and begins to tap her foot. I have bored a lot of women in my life, and I know the signs.

I fix Sam with my most sincere stare and hope that it doesn't come off as creepy. I try to make my voice sound ominous. "And then Indianapolis happened, and everything changed."

"Oh yeah that was so sad. So many young soldiers turned into zombies in Indianapolis. But how did that affect you?" She stares at me with big brown eyes, full of inquisitive energy. I think I might have gotten her attention again.

"Well, it all started one day in Mid-October," I begin, hoping that Sam never took her eyes off me again.

■■

Laying on the couch, I beg Ackmed to let us watch something else, but he refuses, raising the remote in a silent show of victory.

Kevin gestures with his hands in the universal sign for I give up. "At least pick a station so we can pay attention."

I stand up. "There are no women even broadcasting. Let's watch a DVD or something. I'll go get Star Wars."

Kevin sits up. Sounding suspicious, he asks, "Which one?"

"Well, its six o'clock so we can do one of the trilogies. Either the prequel or the original."

Before I can tell them about the Rif Traxx that I had downloaded, I am pelted with pillows and assailed with screams asking me how I could suggest a night of torture with the prequels.

Ackmed settles back into his chair. "No, we are watching the news. Besides, I found a girl broadcaster."

We all look at the screen. "That's Rachel Madow. You really want to watch her?"

Before Ackmed can answer, a special report bulletin appears. Some broadcaster tells me that he is interrupting my regularly scheduled program for a message from the President. As they go live to the White House, my stomach begins to growl nervously as I anticipate what message we are about to receive. Hopefully, it has nothing to do with us. Maybe we are starting another war or something.

The President is sitting behind his famous desk in the oval office wearing a black tie and suit, as if he is in mourning. His dark face is haggard, and his hair is grayer than I remember. There are lines under his eyes and around his mouth.

"He looks like shit," Kevin observes from my dad's La-Z-Boy. "I wonder why he is so upset."

Ackmed, sitting next to me, snorts. "Maybe he is sad because one of the blue states got taken over by zombies. It is an election year, after all."

The speech continues, interrupting Ackmed. Crossing his hands, he says, "My fellow Americans. This past week, the United States has suffered an unexpected and terrible loss. "

As he leans forward and stares sincerely into the camera, the feeling in my stomach gets worse. "Earlier this week, we lost contact with one of our elite units battling to free the Midwest. All personnel that entered Indianapolis are presumed dead. In light of this event, I have decided to take drastic measures to prevent further tragedy. "

Perhaps for dramatic effect, he pauses. Ackmed makes a manic face and mimics pushing a button. "I hope he isn't going to nuke us, the crazy fucker."

The feeling in my stomach spreads down into my legs as the President continues. "From the beginning of this epidemic, I have assured Americans that our homeland would remain safe. Thanks to the efforts of the brave men and women of our military, as well the dedicated officers of homeland security, we have ended the spread of this terrible virus. It is with great joy that I tell you no new cases have been reported outside the Midwest for the past month."

Removing his glasses, he sighs deeply and sits forward. Eyes downcast, he tells us, "After conversing with our military leaders, I have decided to suspend further advances into the containment area indefinitely. This order will be effective immediately. Even as we speak, the men and women of our armed forces are redeploying and forming a perimeter around the Midwest. "

The camera zooms in really close on the President's face to let us know that he is really upset. "To those of you who are watching from the affected zone, you are in my prayers. To those of you with family in the containment zone, rest assured that when your family members reach our perimeter, they will be given immediate medical treatment, if needed, and put into contact with you as soon as possible. I would like to thank the men and women of the United States Armed Forces, who for the last five months have dedicated themselves to rescuing as many affected people as possible. Your sacrifices and commitment will not be forgotten. God Bless You, and God Bless America. "

The camera fades out. After telling me to stay tuned for in depth political analysis, MSNBC goes to commercial. I shut the TV off. I don't want to hear in depth political analysis from talking heads. It doesn't matter what they say. We aren't going to be rescued.

Ackmed sits on the couch in silence, staring at the dark television like it is still on. Kevin stands up and walks out of the room without a word.

I feel like screaming. Up until that moment, I hadn't realized just how much I want to be rescued. I miss McDonald's, new video games, and good beer. I miss women. I love my friends, but it is kind of a sausage fest here. I want to steal glances at pretty girls when they aren't looking.   I want desperately to meet Hester, to hold her. I want to smell her perfume and run my hands through her hair.

And sleep with her, of course.

Before, this zombie thing had seemed like some kind of grotesque vacation. A side trip into an insane world that I could control. Almost like a dream where I didn't have to worry about things like money and career choices. I could just exist here. Now, it seems like I am no longer on a vacation, but in a prison. I am dreaming and I can't wake up.

Ten minutes ago, I was dreading being rescued, but now I am done with the zombie apocalypse.

■■■

Ackmed and I continue to stare at the blank television. There is nothing to say. Even Ackmed doesn't have a poorly timed, inappropriate joke. There are no movie quotes covering this eventuality.   The only thing from literature that I can think of is Caesar saying, "Et tu Brute?"

But Caesar had died after uttering that. And I don't want to die. But, I am going to. Maybe not today, maybe not tomorrow, but soon. Eventually, we will run out of food to eat, or one of us will get sick or hurt. Or the power will fail. Any number of things could kill us. The zombie apocalypse is a dangerous place.

Ackmed sighs. "Well, we have got to get out."

The thought of escaping has not even crossed my mind. It is roughly 75 miles to Milwaukee, the closest unaffected city. But what exists over those miles? Will the roads be clogged? Will there be more zombies migrating from Chicago? Would we walk those miles? Where would we sleep? Where would we eat? Where could I chat with Hester?

"We can't escape, it's impossible."

"It's not impossible. It's just Milwaukee. We went there last year to watch the Cubs play the Brewers. It's a three hour drive, tops. Then, we are home free."

"Oh, a three hour drive, is that all? Well, let's go then. I'll bring my mitt; maybe we can catch a game. Or better yet, make some new friends along the way and play ball with them. What the fuck is wrong with you? This is the fucking apocalypse, not some Sunday afternoon trip to the ballpark. Did you think about the expressways? Did you even read <u>World War Z</u>? They are going to be fucked. Cars and zombies will clog the way, and there will be no easy way on or off. Three hours? We'll be lucky if we last ten minutes. "

"So we are just going to sit here and do what? Wait to die? Make money we can't spend? Have cyber sex with some dude we met online?"

We are so involved in arguing with each other that neither of us notices Kevin leaning on the doorway until he speaks. "Wait a sec. I got an idea."

Ackmed and I stop arguing and look to Kevin. Kevin has an idea. Not only does Kevin have an idea, but he has presented this idea to us in the voice of Harrison Ford; "I got an idea," is a direct quote from the end <u>of Return of the Jedi</u>. Movie quotes mean that we are back in business.

Sounding like a Zen Master, Kevin tells us, "To go up, you must first go down." I want to tell him to get to the point, but I don't want to ruin his moment. He looks like a kid bringing his first A home to his parents.

"To reach your destination, you must first head away from it." Kevin pushes his hands apart and closes his eyes, humming like a meditating monk.

Ackmed decides to ruin the moment. "What do you mean?"

"Exactly that." Kevin sounds proud of himself. "We'll head southwest. About 25 miles from here, it becomes farmland. Once we get into that farmland, we can head west a bit, and shoot up the middle of the state on back roads. It's mostly farmland there anyway. There shouldn't be that many zombies."

It is the zombie apocalypse, and we are back in business.

Six

"It sounded so simple at the time," I tell Sam. To my pleasure, she leans forward in her chair again. "Just west of us was the country. I'm talking farms and cows. With no people to be infected, there wouldn't be any zombies. Ackmed thought we might even be able to stop and do some cow tipping."

Laughing, Sam asks, "Have you ever actually tipped a cow?"

"Nope. The country was near me, but I am a suburbanite born and raised."

She puts her hand on my arm again, spreading warmth throughout my body. "Good. I couldn't ever go for a guy that was country enough to tip a cow."

I continue to explain our preparations to Sam, who leans forward and looks deep into my eyes. Fighting against her penetrating gaze, I describe how we loaded up my parents Volkswagen Tiguan with cans of vegetables, jars of peanut butter, and boxes of Macaroni and Cheese.

Sam arches an eyebrow. "Blue box or yellow?"

I hesitate before answering. This is a big question. I love blue box Mac and Cheese, the kind that kids eat. Not many grownups are as passionate about their choice of Mac and Cheese as I am. I expect the fantasy that I have created about Sam to collapse, but I have to be honest.

"Blue." I hold my breath in anticipation of her answer.

Sam nods solemnly. "Especially the kind with the fun shapes."

Blue box Mac and Cheese with fun shapes can make a marriage. Before I am forced to declare my love for Sam, I continue my story. "We backed up all of our hard drives to the cloud and loaded the car with weapons and ammo. The more we packed, the easier it sounded. I became convinced that once we got out in the country, we wouldn't even see a zombie. The whole journey began to take on the air of a college road trip. Kevin even downloaded a bunch of Smodcasts to listen to on the trip."

I leave out the part about my last passionate chat with Hester. I feel that it is better not to tell Sam about some of the things that Hester had promised to do to me.

"I got the farewell letter on the website. It was really sweet of you to tell the fans what was going on." Sam's voice is magical and I like the way that she says the word sweet.

"Well, we didn't want to leave you guys hanging. We love our fans."

I smile, and Sam rubs my arm some more, using her fingers to tickle me. I pretend that I don't hate being tickled and laugh too. "So did you like the country, Mr. Suburbanite?"

Knowing that it would stop the god awful tickling, I reply. "I didn't go. The morning we were planning to leave, the President called."

∎∎∎

The sound of the phone ringing startles me. Since the phones have not worked in months, when we hear an odd ringing noise, it is hard to place at first. The phone is ringing. I reflect on the oddity of that.

All three of us stare at the ringing phone sitting on the end table in my living room. A ringing phone is no big deal, but when you haven't heard one for a while, it really makes you think. The ring itself is loud and shrill, like some sort of warning system screaming at you over and over again. *Someone wants to talk to you. Someone wants to talk to you.* It gets your attention. And the phone itself. What a wonder of modern technology. It is capable of reaching almost anyone on the planet for any reason. From saying hello to ordering a pizza to phone sex, a phone is an amazing device when you really think about it. Try going without one for a couple of months, and you will see what I mean.

Kevin manages to overcome his surprise a bit, and performs a terrible impersonation of Steve Buschemi. "Your phone's ringing dude."

My Jeff Bridges is not very good either. Too nervous to sound exasperated, I reply, "Thank you, Kevin."

I pick up the receiver and stare at it. I need to remember how to answer it. A phone is complicated, and there are so many buttons. Thankfully, one of them is cleverly labeled talk, so I push that one. "Hello?"

A man's voice answers. It is deep and loud without trying, like a weight lifter. "Is this Malcolm Tushton? Born 08/24/82?"

"This is him. May I ask who is calling please?" I am being oddly formal and polite, like when someone calls that you suspect is a telemarketer, but you aren't quite sure. The same feeling I got when I watched the President's speech the week before begins to creep into my stomach.

"This is Agent Bradshaw, Secret Service. I have the President of the United States standing by for you. Please hold while I connect you." I begin to sweat and my legs get weak. My stomach starts doing jumping jacks.

I hear a click, and then light rock begins to play. The music actually calms me down, and I start to wrap my mind around the idea that I am on hold for the President. I begin to pay attention to the music. It sucks. I can't believe that the White House actually has hold music. I begin to giggle, and Ackmed looks confused as he mouths, "What?"

"They are playing Michael Bolton," I reply, still giggling.

"Who's playing Michael Bolton?"

"The President. " I am being purposely coy. I am the writer of the group, so I control the story, and I love every minute of it. Delayed gratification.

Kevin cannot take the anticipation any more. "Of the United States?"

"Yep. Well, the White House . I am on hold for the Grant Brackley."

I expect Ackmed and Kevin's mouths to actually drop open, but Ackmed ruins my fun. "Well that makes sense. I mean why not. We have zombies, so why wouldn't the President call and make you listen to that no talent ass clown Michael Bolton?"

"He must want something," Kevin concludes, placing his hand under his chin in an impression of The Thinking Man. He sounds calm enough, but I can tell that this whole phone call has Kevin just as spooked as me. He has stated the obvious twice in the last two minutes.

"Of course he wants something. Why else would he call us? Just to chat?" Ackmed seems to be the only person taking the phone call in stride. At the very least, he is responding with the customary angry streak that he has exhibited since his parents died. "Malcolm, you ought to tell that fucker off. He's the reason that we aren't going to be rescued."

Before I can respond, another click sounds and the music stops. I put my finger to my lips in order to shut Ackmed and Kevin up, just as a familiar voice begins talking in my ear. "Mr. Tushton? This is Grant Brackley."

"Um, hello, uh, sir. How are you?" I didn't think that much could faze me after the shit I'd been through in the last couple of months, but talking with the most powerful man in the world is some scary shit.

"I'm fine. How are you?"

I can't believe it. I am making small talk with the President of the United States. What does he want? Could he want a favor from me? As I notice my backpack sitting on the table, I begin to get angry. This man is the reason that I am all packed and ready to go instead of playing video games or sleeping. Why should I do a favor for the man that abandoned me? I decide to listen to Ackmed. "We're fine here, sir. Just another day paradise. Really, the zombie apocalypse is like a vacation. You should try it."

He doesn't rise to my bait. "I bet that you are wondering why I am calling you."

"Well, the thought had occurred to me, sir. And I've got to say, while I did vote for you, I am not going to be able to make a donation to your reelection campaign. I support your healthcare reform policy, but I am very much against your leaving my friends and me to die policy. But I do appreciate your very personal way of soliciting funds. It's novel."

The words are out of my mouth before I think about it. The problem with being a smart ass is that sometimes you forget to think about whom you are talking to before you talk. Ackmed laughs, but Kevin just shakes his head and looks at the ground.

Brackley doesn't respond for a moment or two, giving me long enough to think about the fact that I had just mocked the most powerful man in the world. Then, he begins to chuckle. His voice stops sounding authoritative, and begins to sound just like a regular guy talking on the phone. "You really do have balls, don't you?"

"About the biggest pair you've ever seen, sir."

He laughs again. "Good. It's good that you have balls."

"I'm a fan of them, sir. My balls, I mean." Ackmed cracks up laughing, while Kevin slaps his forehead. I am talking with the Most powerful man on Earth about my balls. It's like an odd plot point in a bad comedy book.

"I'm sure. And, while I am not calling about a campaign donation, your money is always welcome. I want to explain to you why I stopped the advance. So you know the rationale behind, as you put it, 'the leaving you and your friends to die policy.'"

"Are you calling everyone to tell them why they are being left out in the cold? Because that's going to take a long time. Don't you have the country, or rather some of the country, to run?"

To his credit, President Brackley doesn't sound angry. "No, I am not calling everyone, but we will get to that in a second. Why do you think I stopped the advance?"

"Because the 101st Airborne got destroyed in Indianapolis." The answer is obvious. Does he think that I don't watch the news?

"No. That's the reason we told the public we were stopping the advance. The real reason is we weren't finding survivors in the areas that we cleared. The entire time in Indiana, we rescued barely 2,000 people. Our military lost just over 1,500 soldiers. That's before Indianapolis, mind you. My experts here estimate that the entire quarantine area has a little over 25,000 people left in it. That number drops every day. It took us three months to get about 1/5th of the area cleared, and we suffered that many casualties. Even before we found out how bad the major cities are, we anticipated that we were going to lose more people than we saved. With the airborne division's casualties, we have already lost almost the projected number of survivors. And, as I said, that number gets smaller and smaller every day. From an acceptable loss standpoint, it just isn't feasible to rescue anyone else. The destruction of the airborne just gave us a good political excuse to stop the advance."

He is beginning to sound like a politician again, using words like "feasible," and "acceptable losses." I don't like it.

" We told people that the military needed to go through a retraining program in order to be able to adequately defend itself against the undead, and that we would resume rescue efforts when that was completed. While our military does need training in killing these things, the part about resuming the rescue effort is bullshit. We are not coming into your area any time soon, if ever."

The President has just admitted to lying to me. Better than that, he has called his own speech bullshit. No politician ever admitted to lying, especially so candidly. Maybe I should go into journalism instead of novel writing. I am a great interviewer.

"Do you understand where I am coming from Malcolm? Why I made the decision that I did?"

I want to be mad at him, but with the reasoning he gave me, it is kind of hard to. It makes sense. The needs of the many outweigh the needs of the few. "I understand. Even though it kind of sucks for me, I think that you made the right choice. And, let me say, I am sorry that I was such a smart ass before."

Eating crow is never easy, but it is easier to do when you are eating it in front of the President.

"Don't worry about it. I would have probably reacted the same way, had I been in your shoes. I thought that you were actually somewhat restrained in what you said. And, for what it is worth, I am sorry that I had to strand you and your friends there."

Surprisingly, I find myself liking this man. He sounds sincere. In an attempt to reassure him, I tell him, "I wouldn't worry about it too much, sir. I think that we have a really solid escape plan. We'll be fine."

The President's voice sounds casual. "Does that mean I can count on your donation when you get out?"

Now I know I like him. He is a smart ass.

I want to ask for an ambassador's appointment, but he interrupts me. "Before I go on, I want you to stop calling me sir. It is important to know that for the rest of this conversation, I am no longer your President. I am just a guy named Grant who is asking you for a favor."

"Ok, Grant. Call me Malcolm. What's up?" I am getting more and more comfortable talking to him. Maybe I should go into politics instead of journalism.

"I am going to be frank. You can still be Malcolm. I called to ask you to rescue my wife. She's been trapped inside my house with some secret service agents since this whole thing began."

I don't know what to say. I knew that there had to be something he wanted, because the President doesn't call nerds like me just to exchange dirty jokes. Even if I am hilarious.

"Are you there, Malcolm?" He sounds concerned that I might hang up.

"I'm here, sir," I manage whisper. My mind is racing, trying to figure out angles and possibilities. Grant lives in Hyde Park, which is in Chicago. Zombietown, USA.

"Can you help me? Can you save her?" He sounds like he is pleading with me.

"Why me, sir? I'm just a computer tech. Don't you have Navy Seals or someone that could do this for you?

"Stop calling me sir, Malcolm. To answer your question, I can't send a team of Navy Seals to rescue her. It wouldn't be right. I just issued an order stopping any and all rescue attempts. There can be no exceptions to that rule. Not me, not you, and not my wife."

His voice broke a bit as he said the word wife, and I can't help but feel bad for the guy. His wife is trapped, and he has all the resources in the world available to him, but his consciousness won't let him rescue her.

Composing himself, he continues. "That's why you have to call me Grant. That's why you have to realize that during this conversation, I am asking you to help me, Mr. Grant Brackley, not President Grant Brackley. You have to know that if you agree to this, there will be no reward from the federal government, and if you don't agree to do it, there will be no punishment either."

That speech sounds like something he had practiced. He comes off as the lawyer he is, with carefully crafted words. It does sound honest, however.

Then he does something that lawyers never do. He gives me the full story. "I want to tell you exactly what type of situation they are in. I don't want you to make a decision without all the facts."

When he is finished explaining, he again sounds desperate. "Can you help me?"

I want to help him. I like him. He sounds honest and moral, which is an odd way to describe a politician. "I can't make that decision alone, Grant. There are two other people here that I need to speak with. Is there a number that I can call you back at?"

After writing down Grant's personal cell phone number, I hang up the phone and stare at it for a while. Behind me, Kevin and Ackmed are practically jumping up and down with anticipation. I turn and stare at them. This is going to be a hard sell. It is essentially a suicide mission, with no benefits. All risk and no reward.

How can I convince them to come with me? We all have bright futures ahead of us. Kevin wants to make movies.   Ackmed is brilliant on camera. He is both funny and charming. All modesty aside, I am a pretty good writer. We are all relatively internet famous, and we could use that fame to go to Hollywood and make a lot of money.

Or we could go to Chicago and probably die.

Seven

"What did he want?" Kevin's voice is a few octaves higher than normal, like a teenager going through puberty.

As Grant had with me, I decide to be frank. They can still be Ackmed and Kevin. "He wants us to save his wife."

Neither Ackmed nor Kevin say anything, they just stare at me. Trying to make it sound conversational, I say, "She is trapped with a few secret service agents in Hyde Park."

"What, now he needs our help? After he left us here? Why did you even bother to ask us? Why not tell him straight out to go fuck himself?" Ackmed's voice is a few octaves lower than normal, like the growl of an angry animal.

"Ackmed, it's not that simple. Look he had his-"

"And why were you so nice to him at the end of that phone call? Yes sir, no sir, how about a blowjob, sir, being as your wife is about to become a zombie?"

It's like I am not even speaking to anyone at all. Ackmed continues to yell, slamming everyone from the President for abandoning us to the army for being incompetent. Kevin eases a bit closer to me and whispers, "You know how he gets. Let him finish, and then you can talk."

I have seen this side of Ackmed before. He will rant until he either gets tired, runs out of things to say, or has to go to the bathroom. I use the time to think about a strategy to convince my friends to commit what amounts to suicide. Right around the time Ackmed begins calling the Secret Service "the retarded Men in Black," I decide what I need to say. As I fine tune my arguments, Ackmed concludes, "And to think I voted for that spineless coward."

He pauses, breathing heavily. His face is red and he is sweating, exhausted from the sheer act of speaking. I am not sure how long his tirade went on, but I know that it is long enough to make the silence now permeating the room noticeable.

I have a window while Ackmed catches his breath. I tell him and Kevin what Grant had said to me about the advance. Kevin appears to listen with interest, and looks sad when I tell him how few people in the containment zone have been found alive. "It's like the entire Midwest has been wiped off the map," he says, running his hands through his hair. "A whole cultural group completely destroyed."

I can't tell what Ackmed is thinking. As I speak, he listens impassively, perhaps digesting what I am saying, or perhaps too tired from his speech to speak. Either way, it doesn't matter to me, because what I am saying is meant for Kevin, not Ackmed.

This is the first part of the strategy. I have to convince Kevin. Once he is on my side, then the two of us can try to convince Ackmed together. Kevin's interest in psychology gave him insights into what motivated people, and he could use those insights to help me win Ackmed over.

I once took a writing class where the teacher told me that the best writers understand their characters completely, and that they write actions that are consistent with what their characters wanted. That means understanding their desires and motivations. He suggested that we observe the behavior of people in our personal lives and then analyze that behavior. If we could realize why real people acted a certain way, then we could easily use that knowledge to help us build real characters.

I am good at it. I don't know if I am the best writer, but I am pretty good. And while I have no idea what motivates Ackmed, I know exactly what motivates Kevin. Kevin wants to help people desperately. When we went into Chicago for Cubs games, he gave the homeless guys money. He was trying to talk my dad into fostering dogs that had been abused. Part of the reason Kevin wants to be a psychologist is that he has an almost unlimited capacity for empathy. I know this about him, and I intend to use it. I am not proud of this, and I hate to think that I am manipulating one of my best friends into doing something suicidal, but I see no other way to convince either of them to help me.

Sometimes, being a great writer means being a shitty human being.

"And that brings us to Crystal." I deliberately use the First Lady's name to make her seem more human.

"When the outbreak happened, Crystal was in Chicago to visit her aunt, who was dying of cancer at the University of Chicago. She wanted to say good bye." Although this is technically all true, the Grant told me the real reason for Crystal's visit was to solicit campaign donations. I leave that part out, focusing on the dying aunt.

I am such an asshole.

"Since the zombies came, she has been trapped inside her house. She has two secret service agents with her. Both of them have families waiting back in Washington." I am not sure about that last part, but I go with it. It increases the sympathy factor, and there is a good chance that the agents really do have family. In all likelihood, we will probably be dead long before we ever meet them, so that little white lie doesn't matter.

Except that it makes me hate myself just a little bit more.

"Grant is asking us to help get his wife to Milwaukee. He loves her very much, and issuing the order that abandoned her here broke his heart."

I am afraid for a moment that I laid it on too thick, but Kevin's eyes glisten with emotion. I know that I have him. "That is so sad, man. Where do we come in?"

Meet Malcolm Tushton, manipulative fuck and world's worst best friend.

I quickly add the moral reasons why the military cannot get involved before Ackmed can jump on Kevin for using the word we.

"Wow, a moral politician. I didn't think that they existed." Ackmed sounds impressed, and I think for a moment that I have convinced him too. I didn't even need Kevin's help. With an evil grin, Ackmed continues. "Too bad he's not less of an idealist, because it's going to kill his wife. I am sure as hell not going to let one moral crusader get me killed."

Kevin, looking appalled, begins to speak. "Wait a minute. No one is getting anyone killed. Ackmed, you told us once that you wanted to do good, remember? What could be better than rescuing a trapped woman from hordes of zombies? Was that all lip service, or do you really want to do something positive?"

I forgot a lot about our conversation in Mr. Chimelski's basement, but Kevin, the attentive shrink, apparently remembered. He didn't even need to write it down in his notepad.

Ackmed begins to answer, but Kevin ignores him. He is in the zone, on his own rant now. "How dare you mock a man for using his power morally. We need more moral people in power, not less. If people would just worry more about the greater good than their own personal stake in things, this country would be a better place. He should be rewarded for acting like that, not mocked and condemned to wait for his wife's death."

And I thought I had laid it on thick.

"We have a chance to do something good here, something really good. And I don't mean just rescue the President's wife, I mean rescue someone's wife. A person that is loved by someone else. A lover, friend, wife, and mother. We can help to save her. Not just her either. Maybe we will come across some other lost people on our trip. There have got to be at least some survivors out there. We can help them too."

Looking like a puppy that is getting yelled at for peeing on the rug, Ackmed stares down at the carpet. Just when I begin to think that Kevin is getting a bit too mean, he surprises me yet again. "If that's not enough, think about what will happen to us once we rescue the First Lady. We will be famous. And don't tell me that we are famous now; we are internet famous. I mean that we will be really famous. We can go on all the talk shows and do interviews. Malcolm can probably write a book for each of us. It will sell. People love to read about the newest hero.

Remember that Sully guy that landed the plane in the river? He wrote a book, and he's rich now. On top of that, he has been interviewed on every network station there is."

Leaning in towards Ackmed, Kevin takes the selfishness to a new level. "Can you imagine the tail that guy must get? Do you think for a minute that Sully didn't fuck Meredith Viera before he went on the Today Show? I bet that she went down on her knees faster than that fucking plane fell from the sky into that river."

Ackmed has a huge crush on Meredith Viera. Apparently, Kevin can be just as manipulative as me. I can see from Ackmed's widening eyes that it is working. Hell, even I begin to picture Jenna Lee from *Fox News* naked. I hate *Fox News*, but find that as long as I keep the sound off, I can watch when Jenna Lee is on the air.

"Plus, I bet we can use this to get some of our movies made. What studio executive would turn down three American heroes? Look at Audie Murphy after World War II. He was a movie star."

Ackmed begins to get into the festive spirit too. Shaking his head in wonderment, he points out, "Having the most powerful man on earth owe us a solid isn't exactly a bad thing either. I bet we can make a whole list of demands, you know Armageddon style. I don't ever want to pay taxes again either, just like Bruce Willis."

I hate to rain on their parade, but at this point, I have to. This is something that I cannot lie to them about. Not only had Grant stressed it with me, but they are my friends. "There won't be any list. If we do this, it is not for the President Grant Brackley, it is for the private citizen Grant Brackley. The government has no part in this, other than to open the phone lines."

They look confused, so I explain to them the finer points of the separation of powers that Grant had told me about. I am afraid that the idea has completely soured when Ackmed says, "Shit if there is no obvious benefit to it, then we will look even more heroic. Bring on Meredith."

Everyone is in. Now we just have to figure out how to do it.

Eight

"Are you hitting on me?" Sam moves her arm away from mine and leans back in her chair. Her brown eyes rage like a storm.

"No, why would you say that?" Panic edges into my voice.

"Well, I get a lot of guys in here hitting on me, telling me that they are friends with important people. None have been stupid enough to refer to the President by his first name, though. Look, if you wanted to impress me, you have impressed me with your writing. The fact that you know about elves is a bonus. But you don't need to add in something about the President." Folding her arms across her chest, she purses her lips. Leaning farther back in her chair, she stares at me coldly.

As she is already angry, I didn't think that it would be an appropriate time to stare at her thighs, which become visible as she leans backwards. After looking only a little, I jump to my feet, speaking quickly. "Wait wait, it's the truth, I swear. Listen to the story. I am not trying to impress you at all."

She sighs loudly and begins to stand. My brain rushes along frantically, trying to think of the right words. "Ok, maybe I am trying to impress you a little, Sam. A lot, even. How many cute girls do think I meet with have elfish tattoos?"

She can't hide her smile when I mention her tattoo. Sitting back down, she looks at me closely, squinting her eyes. She points her finger at me. "Ok, but no more bullshit."

"I don't know how to say this so that you will believe me, but it wasn't bullshit at all. Ok maybe I wasn't quite that rude to the President, but he did call. I swear." It sounds pathetic and whiney even to me. Nothing turns a woman on more than a guy whining.

Sighing again and rolling her eyes, her voice takes on that skeptical tone that all women have mastered. "So what happened next? Did you rush off to save Mrs. Brackley?"

"Not right away. There was something that we had to take care of first."

■■

The three of us stand outside of a familiar two story blue house. Around us, nothing moves, not even the wind. The grass is overgrown, but brown and dying because it is late October. A chill causes me to shiver a bit under my Red vs. Blue hoodie. It's stylish, but could be a bit warmer.

Looking at Ackmed, Kevin says, "Are you sure that you want to do this?"

Ackmed hesitates, and then nods. We walk past the dying grass and up the concrete driveway. I shiver again, and Kevin looks concerned. Ackmed only stares straight ahead, not glancing left or right. He holds a shotgun in his hand. Kevin and I both carry pistols.

The screen door opens with a creak, but the door doesn't move when Ackmed pushes it. "It's locked," he says sheepishly and reaches into his pocket for his keys. His hands are shaking, and he drops them. Cursing, he picks the keys up and puts them in the door. They turn smoothly and the door opens.

I know the inside of the house as well as the outside. The hallway has a shiny white linoleum floor leading directly into the kitchen. On the right, a wooden staircase leads upstairs to the bedroom. A smaller staircase running parallel to the first leads to another family room. To our left is a carpeted family room with old, dusty furniture sitting in it.

Ackmed calls out, "Mom? Dad?"

Predictably, no one answers. Walking forward, Ackmed calls out again, then stands in front of the lower staircase. To his left, a three foot wide opening in the wall connects the kitchen and the basement family room. It also allows a clear view of the lower level. Ackmed cries out, and steps back from the stairs. Kevin and I raise our guns into the ready stance we learned on TV, but Ackmed just stands by the stairs. He drops his shotgun, which hits the white ceramic tile with a thud that cracks the floor.

A moan escapes the basement, just as Ackmed sinks to a sitting position. As I move closer, I see tears streaming down his dark face. He points. Peering through the opening in the wall, I see Mr. and Mrs. Sharma. Their skin is now gray, and their eyes dark. Both of them wear pajamas. Not sweats and t-shirts, but honest to God pajamas, like Dick Van Dyke and Mary Tyler Moore. Mr. Sharma has noticed us, and is trying to climb the four stairs up to the second level, arms outstretched. He can't seem to figure out the how the staircase works. Mrs. Sharma, no longer pretty, doesn't notice us at all. She appears to be trying to get at a squirrel which is sitting outside the window. She doesn't even turn to look at us, but instead walks into the window over and over again.

I don't know what to say. Ackmed breaks the uncomfortable silence. "I don't think that I can do it."

Raising my pistol, which suddenly feels very heavy, I take aim at the top of Mr. Sharma's head. He has a bald spot on the back of his skull, which will serve as some sort of target for me. My hand shakes. I try to pull the trigger, but nothing happens. I try again to pull the trigger, but the gun again refuses to go off. It is as if my mind will not allow my body to perform this terrible act. Mr. and Mrs. Sharma are different than any other zombie couple I have ever seen. I have known them since I was a little kid. Mrs. Sharma went from being a nice lady that made us cheese sandwiches to someone to tease Ackmed about with 'yo mamma jokes.' At the end of high school, her beauty tortured my dreams and I found myself unable to look her in the eyes when she returned from her daily runs wearing nothing but a spandex sports bra and tight pants.

While Mr. Sharma was more distant and not nearly as sexual, he had still always been a constant in my life. When I was a kid, we used to play with matchbox cars and GI Joes together. In high school, he helped me with my science homework.

All of these memories and more flash through my mind all at once. I lower my gun too. Surprised to find tears in my eyes, I tell Ackmed, "I can't do it either."

We both look at Kevin, who shakes his head sadly. If we can't do it, he for sure can't. We sit there on the stairs for a long time, Ackmed crying and me trying to endure the silence. After an eternity, Ackmed stands up. "Let's go," he tells us in a sure voice.

I take one last long hard look at the Sharma's house and walk out the door.

NINE

"And that is not bullshit at all." I wipe my wet eyes. It's a mean thing to say, but Sam did accuse me of lying to her.

Her brown eyes are wide circles. For some reason she is crying too. Standing up, she gives me a hug. She is soft in my arms, and warm. Her hair feels good on my face. She apologizes for doubting me, then hugs me harder. "You poor thing."

"It's ok," I say, sniffling. "It's a pretty outlandish story."

I continue to hug her, enjoying the warmth of her body and softness of her skin. Eventually, biology combined with those sensations causes me to break the hug off, lest she slap me. The only thing less sexy than a man whining is a man crying. That or a really hairy guy.

"What happened to Ackmed?" Sam asks, sitting down again but keeping her hand over mine. Her grip is strong yet gentle all at the same time. Her skin is so smooth, so different from my own.

"He was pretty quiet for the rest of the day, but the next morning, he woke up as if nothing happened. He wanted to talk about supplies and planning our mission. He refused to talk about his parents with us. So we just threw ourselves into planning the trip into the city."

Sam doesn't reply, but she doesn't move her hand either. I can tell that she is still skeptical about the President, so I push on quickly before she can think about it. "We stole a lot of supplies from our neighbors, and a lot of guns from a nearby gun store. We doubled our supply of food and water, loading it all into a bright yellow Nissan Pathfinder that we nicknamed "Insanity." It took about two weeks to get the entire trip set up, but in early November, we were ready to go."

■■

"Let's kick the tires and light the fires." Ackmed sits behind the wheel of Insanity, gripping the steering wheel. He has on sunglasses, camouflage BDU pants, and a hoodie with the words, 'No I will not fix your computer,' on the front. He looks like a cross between an outsourced computer tech and a terrorist.

"Let's do it." Kevin sits in the back seat. He is dressed identically to Ackmed, except his black shirt reads, 'ID10T error."

"I'm recording," Kevin says, quite unnecessarily. We can see that his flip camera is out, a little red dot in glowing in the front. He turns the camera around so that it will record his face and gives us his best over dramatic starship captain. "Star date November 9th 2011: Our mission is to rescue the First Lady."

I am sitting shotgun, with a GPS on the dash, water in the cup holder, and a rifle at my feet. I am also wearing BDU pants, but I have on a black T-shirt with a picture of a shotgun and the words 'ask me about my zombie plan,' printed on it. Pointing to Ackmed, I say, "Red 5 standing by. Punch it Chewie."

Everyone is too nervous to point out that Han Solo was never Red 5, and that Chewie couldn't even fit inside an Xwing. We are leaving our home, our safety net. And while Insanity is strong, it will never be as safe as home. All of us are a bit subdued, wondering if the planning and preparation that has occurred in the last two weeks has been enough.

Making our way quickly through town, Ackmed pauses at the intersection of Archer Road and McCarthy. He looks from Kevin to me. "Well, here we are. Left will take us northeast into the city, and right will take us southwest to safety. You sure about this?"

I am not so sure anymore. Rescuing Crystal had sounded like a good idea two weeks ago, but as we drive through the abandoned streets of my hometown, I feel like I am going to throw up. When Ackmed asks which way I want to turn, my heart begins to beat so hard that it threatens to shake itself out of my chest and run away down the street.

This whole adventure is my idea. If anything happens to Kevin or Ackmed, it will be my fault. Not only had I schemed to convince them to come, but I am kind of the leader of our little band. As the writer of the group, I decide the plot. That's a lot of responsibility.

I want this story to end happily ever after, not with everyone dying. Or ambiguously like a lot of modern books. I like happy endings, and not just when getting massages. The problem with this story is that the easiest way to achieve a happy ending is to turn right.

"Of course we go left. We've spent the last two weeks preparing for this. Let's do it." As he speaks, Kevin licks his lips but shows no other signs of being nervous.

"Ok, here we go." Ackmed sounds disappointed, like he was hoping that we would change our minds.

As we turn, Kevin sings. "There's no place I'd rather be, since I found Insanity."

We accelerate up to speed and quickly pass the Cog Hill Golf Course, where the US Open would be taking place had there not been any zombies. The roadside becomes thick with trees as we enter the giant forest preserve north of town.

"I'm getting a great feed off of all the cameras. They are recording onto the hard drive, and onto the flash drive. This is going to be a great movie." Kevin had set up several digital cameras in different directions all over the Insanity in order to get a full 360 degree view.

The lack of traffic and movement would have been weirder, except that over the course of the last few months, we have gotten used to being the only living creatures around. As we passed the Willowbrook Ballroom, where the ghost of Resurrection Mary is rumored to appear to male drivers, a hideous moan shatters the silence. Nothing moves, and we speed past the building. Ackmed tells us that he saw a flash of white that suddenly disappeared, but Kevin and I decide that it must have been a zombie moaning. We keep driving, although a few minutes later when we pass Resurrection Cemetery, where Mary is buried, Ackmed speeds up again. Beads of sweat form on his forehead.

"No time to worry about legends. We have real monsters to fight." I try to sound tough, but I am not sure if it comes out right.

Eventually, Ackmed slows down. We continue up Archer Avenue, passing small houses set back from the road.

"We are making great time," Ackmed rolls down his window and puts his hand out of it.

I don't answer right away. While I am not incredibly superstitious, I don't want to tempt fate. Still, it is a beautiful afternoon, with just enough sun to keep you comfortably warm. Although the trees have already lost their leaves, the forest still makes for pretty scenery.

"We might be able to make it into Hyde Park tomorrow or the next day." Kevin's optimism terrifies me. However, it is only noon and we have already traveled farther than we expected to go the entire day.

I notice Ackmed's mouth beginning to open. "Don't say it, Ackmed."

He ignores me and cracks half a smile. "This is looking easier and easier. Maybe it isn't a suicide mission."

I look aghast, and shake my head. "No need to tempt fate."

"Look Malcolm. Nothing happened. This isn't an action movie, this is real life." Ackmed's mouth drops open and his eyes widen. "Oh my God, look at that."

Even as I turn, I hear Kevin and Ackmed laughing. The only thing in the direction that Ackmed indicated is a sign that reads, "Welcome to Summit."

"We are in Summit, Malcolm. Oh the humanity."

Summit is a little town bordering the City of Chicago. The town has always looked kind of shady, with older buildings and graffiti on the walls. There was always a building that had been burned out or a house with boards over the windows. And that was before the apocalypse.

Now, half the block is missing, burned to the ground. The rest of the homes have broken windows. It looks as if the citizens of Summit had responded to the crisis by rioting.

A man wanders through the rubble, swaying with the all too familiar walk of one of the infected. He wears a Bears shirt and jeans. Hearing our truck, Bears Fan turns toward us and limps in our direction.

Ackmed slows the car to a stop. The man is in the middle of the street now, about 25 feet away.

"I think that it would be best to do something hand to hand, here." Ackmed unbuckles his safety belt. "I don't want to damage the truck."

Ackmed gets out of the truck and leans in. "Kevin, are you getting this?"

Kevin nods, and Ackmed begins to advance toward Bears Fan.

I got out too, carrying the same pistol that I had shot Andy with. Ackmed is good, but I want to back him up, just in case. Safety first.

When he is about three feet away from the zombie, Ackmed attacks. Rather than use his strength to decapitate Bears Fan, Ackmed decides to use finesse. Holding the tip of his sword so that it is level with Bears Fan's right eye, Ackmed grunts and pushes it forward. Entering the eye cavity, the sword exits out the back of Bear's Fan's head. Blood runs from the wound as his shattered eyeball splits in two pieces and falls to the ground.

Nothing else changes. The zombie still advances towards Ackmed, who stares dumbfounded at his failure. He still holds the hilt of the sword. Bracing himself, he pulls with his entire strength on the sword, which doesn't move.

Ackmed appears to be so surprised that he stands frozen the street holding the sword and swearing.

"Ackmed, back up," I shout aiming my pistol.

Bear's Fan advances forward even as he continues to impale himself further. Once the entire blade is sticking out the back of his skull, he moans and leans close to Ackmed. Placing my pistol against the zombie's forehead, I pull the trigger. Bear's Fan falls to the ground so quickly that the sword rips through the top of his skull, covering Ackmed with gray brains and dark blood.

"Well that didn't go well." Kevin slams his camera shut.

Ackmed shakes his head and wipes some brain matter off of his t-shirt. "Thanks, Malcolm. Now I owe you one."

I don't say anything as he bends to pick up his sword. Wiping it clean on Bears Fan's shirt, he tells me, "It must have gotten stuck on the bastards head. Next time, I will have to-"

I never find out what he will have to do next time, because just then, Kevin screams, "Zombies." His voice is high and panicked, like a man on the edge of the control.

"I know, Kevin. There are zombies. We are living in the zombie apocalypse." Ackmed speaks slowly, like he is explaining something to a particularly dumb child.

As Ackmed and I turn back to the truck, the reason for Kevin's panic is obvious. Advancing behind us is a horde of zombies.

TEN

To call the mass of flesh moving behind us a horde would be the classic definition of an understatement. There are hundreds of them, a giant wave of meat and bone swaying back and forth as they move ever onward. The crowd is so densely packed that if not for the flashes of different colored clothing, it would be hard to pick out individuals. They are individuals, of course, but move together in like step, as if they are some nightmare army on parade.

As like as they are in step, they are also of like mind. All of them want to eat my friends and me. They don't even need to be great thinkers or have a grand strategy. No subtly is needed to overwhelm and eat us.

We sprint to the truck. Ackmed drives far too quickly as we attempt to leave the undead horde far behind us. As we tear down Archer Avenue, the houses become more closely packed and the streets become more crowded with stalled cars. Ackmed weaves Insanity in and out of traffic, narrowly missing parked cars, street signs, and the occasional lone zombie wandering around in the street. As I am thrown around the interior of the truck, I begin to feel dizzy, like when I was 12 and rode the Gravatron too many times at the Keepataw Days Carnival.

"Holy shit that's a lot of fucking zombies," Kevin stutters as we cross Harlem Avenue, barely missing a blue Geo Metro that someone had abandoned in the street.

I don't reply. There are so many zombies, more than I had ever imagined in one place. More than we can kill. More than we can even fight through to safety. For what feels like a long time, the only thing my mind can register is the lurching of the truck and the hundreds of undead approaching me, jaws dripping with saliva.

"Can you see them anymore? Are they gone?" Ackmed is driving so fast that he can't take his eyes off the road to look back.

Turning around and peering out the back window, Kevin says, "No, I don't see them. We must have outrun them.

Ackmed slows to 20 MPH. Sweat drips from his forehead, and his arms shake. "They stopped for now, but as soon as we stop, they can catch up to us."

I am usually not the voice of pessimism, but I can't shake the feeling of doom I got from seeing that number of zombies. Kevin was right; that was a lot of fucking zombies. And they are all going to eat us.

"We have a huge lead on them. They won't ever catch up to us." Kevin sounds the way a child does when they say something in the hope that it will come true.

"Relax, guys, I think I have this figured out." Ackmed wipes sweat from his eyes. "That was a lot of zombies, right? There were easily thousands of them. That means that there are thousands of south side zombies behind us, right?"

No one answers his obvious question, so he continues. "If all the zombies on the south side are behind us, then what is in front of us?"

"Nothing." Kevin sounds proud.

"Exactly. Nothing. Zip. Nada. No one. And, as long as we don't stop, we are safe. So don't worry about it guys, we are good."

We had fought our way into the city, blasting though the zombies' first line of defense. Who knows, maybe all of the zombies in the city were behind us at this point. If so, they would not be able to catch us, just like Ackmed said. My fear begins to fade, and I sit straighter as the confidence begins to run through my veins. I feel strong, like I can take on the whole Empire myself. I begin to think that it is silly to fear the slow, stumbling crowd of zombies. They are lethargic, stupid beasts, while we are quick, smart humans. We are moving so quickly away from them that they probably won't ever catch us.

The truck slams to a stop and I am thrown forward in my seat. I begin to reflect on the wisdom of putting on a seatbelt as Ackmed screams, "Shit."

Streaming down the four lane road that is Archer Avenue, another horde of zombies appears. They begin to march towards us like a grotesque parade. Ackmed throws the car into reverse and turns the wheel. We spin around so quickly that it makes my head hurt, but when the spinning ends we are pointed back in the direction that we came from.

"There are zombies that way," Kevin says helpfully.

"There are zombies behind us too," I scream back.

The truck is stopped, and Ackmed is staring ahead with a half smile on his face. That smile reassures me. Ackmed has a plan. If I am the author and Kevin is the director, then Ackmed is unquestionably the action hero. He will pull some action hero maneuver that I can't think of because it will defy logic, and we will get out of this mess. "What's the plan, Ackmed?"

In answer to my question, Ackmed turns the wheel sharply left and hits the gas. We begin to drive down a residential street. Ackmed continues to smile, but doesn't look left or right. Repeating my question, I tap his arm. His only answer is to drive faster.

As we accelerate down the block, I see zombies struggling towards the street through small gaps between the houses. The gaps aren't large, so there aren't a lot of them yet, but zombies are patient. We need to figure out something, and quickly.

The truck begins to slow again and Kevin demands that Ackmed tell him why we are stopping. Ackmed only points down the block to where the street ends in a giant chain link fence. Behind the fence sits old trucks and construction equipment. One of the problems with the south side is that there are tons of dead end streets, due to all the industrial parks. As our truck stops I can clearly see the yellow sign that reads, 'dead end.'

It seems to be a fitting sign, so full of over the top symbolism that it is almost too obvious. Ackmed turns the truck sideways so that I am facing the doorway of a small brick home with a broken window and Christmas lights on it. "The truck should slow some of the ones in the street down for a bit." Ackmed points at a small blue ranch home about a block away. "I'll do the rest. Go for that last house, the blue on the corner. I'll cover our rear."

His voice is calm. It is the same tone that Ackmed had used in the past describe math problems, ham sandwiches, and the movie 30 Minutes or Less. It is an everyday tone used to describe every day, boring events. Yet this is not an everyday event. Already, little groups of the undead are stumbling across the lawns of various houses. There is no way that he can make it to the blue house before the horde envelopes him. I should be holding them off anyway. I was the one that manipulated him into coming on this adventure. Damn my superior intellect and cunning.

Kevin begins to protest, but Ackmed cuts him off and tells us to move. "If I have to go out, I want to take as many of those bastards with me," he says cocking his shotgun.

Taking off his sunglasses, he opens the door and steps out. "Good luck. You're gonna need it."

The vanguard of the attack is a man wearing overalls that have a Southwest Airlines logo printed on them near the upper right breast. He is easily 15 feet ahead of the crowd. Ackmed raises his shotgun, and with a bang Overall's head disappears. Kevin and I don't move, we only stand there, our jaws dropping. Walking closer to the horde, Ackmed screams, "Go now."

I recognize what is going on and the reality of it combined with the terrible writing makes me want to vomit. Ackmed is sacrificing himself to save us. Ackmed, the character who is the best zombie slayer but will have the most trouble adjusting to normal life, is going to go out with a bang and a terrible catch phrase. It is like something out of a Tom Clancy book, or a terrible action movie. How cliché.

Nonetheless, it would be stupid to let Ackmed's generous act be for naught. Opening the door, I run towards the blue house. I hear Kevin behind me, his footsteps loud thuds on the concrete as he runs. Ackmed's shotgun bangs twice in quick succession. He curses at the zombies, throwing insults as if they are weapons. I want desperately to see what is happening behind me, but I don't dare stop. There are zombies on the street now, reaching for me with gray hands.

Suddenly I am on the porch of the blue house, safe and out of reach of the gray hands. There are now fifteen zombies between me and the truck. I can't see Ackmed, but I know that he is still alive and fighting because I can hear his shotgun as it decapitates zombies.

Kevin is almost at the porch, a shotgun in one hand and a camera in the other. Always the filmmaker, Kevin had taken the extra time to secure his camera. A man wearing a White Sox jersey reaches for him and misses. Kevin smiles then, because the only thing between him and the porch is a red coated black lawn jockey. His smile is replaced by a panicked face as he falls, pitching forward into the grass. His camera and shotgun fly from his hands, landing at the base of the stairs.

White Sox Jersey, followed closely by a Mexican woman, are only steps away. I jump down the stairs, knowing that it is a useless gesture. Kevin is too far away, and the zombies are too close to him. Then, with a sharp crack, White Sox Jersey and Mexican Woman's heads explode.

I pull Kevin to his feet, ignoring the headless corpses. The zombies between the truck and I are beginning to fall with the same high pitched crack that had killed White Sox Jersey and Mexican Woman. I can still hear Ackmed fighting, the deep booms of his shotgun adding to the terrible crescendo of the rifles.

A blond haired boy runs towards us from the yellow house across the street. He has a pistol in his hand and a rifle slung over his shoulder. Pausing in the middle of the street, he fires the pistol directly into a zombies' face. "Come with me to that yellow house. We can't hold them off for too much longer."

He fires the pistol again. There are now only one or two attackers between us and the truck, and they have both lay in the street, struggling to move after tripping over their comrades.

"Our friend is still out there," I scream, running for the truck. I can still hear Ackmed cursing, but the booms of his shotgun have faded.

"I'm coming Ackmed," I yell as I run. "Get back to the truck."

When Ackmed comes into view, he is still about five feet away from me swinging his Katana at a group of three zombies. There are zombies approaching from every direction. Sweat drips from his long dark hair, glistening against his muscled torso in the afternoon sun.

Without thinking, I slide across the hood and land on Ackmed's left. I empty my gun into the crowd, firing again and again. I try to forget about the zombies around me, hoping that Kevin can handle them. I am distantly aware of sounds coming from that area, but the other side of the street may as well have been the other side of the moon for all I cared. Only as I shoved the shotgun into a gray face and hear a click did I jump back and look around.

Behind me, Kevin and the blonde boy are standing behind the truck, using it as a parapet to fire into the crowd. Ackmed and I run to them and fire. Despite the growing pile of zombies behind us and the continuing barks from the rifles, there are zombies behind us again, approaching at a steady pace.

The boy points at a small white home near us. "That one," is all he says as he begins to sprint. Following him, I hear Ackmed swear, but there is no time to look around until I am on in the house. There is a picture window in the front room, and a plasma TV mounted on the wall. A grandfather clock chimes thirteen times. I sink onto orange shag carpet, breathing heavily. Ackmed and Kevin tumble in after me, Ackmed slamming the door behind him. Kevin manages to sit in a leather chair, but Ackmed sits on the linoleum floor next to the door.

The blonde boy is standing at the picture window looking out. He doesn't appear to be phased by the wild run or the escape. There isn't even any sweat on his brow. Struggling to my feet, I begin to stick my hand out, but the boy pushes me to my right and I fall. Pointing the rifle at Ackmed's chest, the blonde says, "Get in the fucking basement now, or I will shoot you myself."

ELEVEN

"What?" Kevin sounds betrayed and confused.

"Back up, and get into the basement. I'm not going to say it again; I am just going to start shooting." Ackmed is already backing down a hallway that leads to stairs. I follow. I hadn't had time to be scared outside because I was too busy, but now I find myself shaking. This boy, for he could be at most sixteen years old, is clearly insane.

"Why would he save us only to shoot us?" Kevin isn't talking to anyone in particular.

The three of us are on the stairs when the boy fires three shots into the wall. We all jump, but continue down the stairs. The basement is a classic homage to mankind. There is a full bar with what appears to be a tap on it. A pool table is in the corner, and a leather couch and chair face a big screen TV. The walls are decorated with posters of various people doing things like breaking tackles, shooting baskets, and throwing footballs. There is no baseball, which is good, because I don't think that I could take the last thing I will see being a White Sox logo. At this point, it is clear that eventually this deranged boy will shoot me.

"Were there zombies in the house?" Kevin, the poor fool, seems more concerned with the zombies than with the boy walking down the stairs holding a smoking gun.

"No." The boy gestures at the leather couch. He sounds softer now, polite and in control. He must be some kind of schizophrenic. "No one was there. Please, sit down."

"I'm not going anywhere." I puff out my chest. I hope that I sound more confident than I feel.

"Well, at least back up. I am not going to hurt anyone; you have to trust me on this." The boy sounds less confident now, almost like a different person. Hopefully this personality will stick around long enough for us to get the gun away from him.

As we move farther into the room, the blonde boy points his rifle at the ground. "See, I mean you no harm. In fact, I just saved your lives twice, if you can believe me. Everyone else will think that I killed you now." The boy offers us a half smile, and adds sheepishly, "I am also a huge fan, and am psyched to meet you."

One of his personalities must like our work. Shrugging, Kevin steps forward and shakes the boy's hand. "I'm Matt. I think that you have a real gift for directing."

"Only because he has good writing to back it up." I shake his hand too. I like this personality. Ackmed doesn't move, so I add, "Of course, we have the best in online talent, so it makes our jobs easy."

Ackmed frowns, and does not acknowledge my compliment. Staring at he boy the way a wolf stares at a deer, he says, "Someone shot at me."

"No, they probably just missed the zombies. They were firing a lot of rounds; it probably just felt that way." Kevin is always ready to believe the best in people.

"No, he's right. They were shooting at him." Matt sounds sad, but then smiles brightly. "I guess that they have been shooting at slow zombies for so long, they forgot how to hit anything moving faster."

"Lucky me," Ackmed responds. We all begin to talk at once. While Kevin asks why anyone would shoot at Ackmed, I inquire as to who the attackers are. Matt apologizes profusely to all of us, practically going on bended knee. Ackmed starts a tirade, but Kevin touches his arm. Ackmed stops talking and the room becomes silent. Indignant silence, but silence none the less.

"Matt, why don't we all have a seat and you can explain. Tell us your story." Kevin gestures at the chair.

"Yeah, sit down and tell me why you and your friends want me dead." Ackmed makes it sound like Matt had tried to kill him. As we sit down, I mouth, "Stop it," to Ackmed. He is being rude, not only to the man who had saved our lives, but to a fan as well.

Matt looks terrified of Ackmed's sudden anger. "They don't want you dead personally."

Before he can continue, Ackmed interrupts him with a snort. "It seemed pretty personal when the bullets were flying by me."

Matt flinches, but doesn't say anything else. "Ackmed, this will only work if you listen. Please don't interrupt Matt again." Kevin sounds more annoyed with Ackmed's anger than normal. "Do please continue Matt."

"Yeah, well, like I said, they, um, don't want you dead personally." Matt is stuttering now, clearly nervous, but manages to continue. Looking away, he says quietly, "They hate all of you people."

Ackmed jumps to his feet before Kevin can say anything. "What do you mean by you people?"

"You know, anyone who isn't white. They actually mainly hate black people. They probably shot at you because they thought you were black."

When no one speaks, Matt continues. "I don't agree with them, in case you were wondering."

"Well, that's good, isn't it Ackmed?" Kevin kicks Ackmed's leg. He nods reluctantly and sits back down.

"Yeah, we are all about tolerance here." Ackmed seems to be choosing his words carefully, struggling to maintain control. "So tell me then Matt, if you don't believe in their views, why are you living with them?"

"I live there because the leader of their group is my father. He's kind of like the Darth Vader to my Luke Skywalker."

Anyone who would reference <u>Star Wars</u> in the middle of the zombie apocalypse is clearly one of our own, and even Ackmed smiles at the comment.

Matt continues, "I also haven't had the inclination to escape. It's too dangerous, with King Thaddeus and all."

"King Thaddeus?"

"Where have you guys been? You don't know about King Thaddeus? He's only the most powerful man in Chicago now. And he hates white people."

"How does he feel about brown people?" Ackmed sounds amused. "He should also change his name. How could I be scared of a guy named Thaddeus?"

"You could, or rather, you should be. If my father is cruel like Darth Vader, Thaddeus is cruel like the Emperor. He has no mercy and no remorse."

None of us were that impressed, so Matt continues. "Let me explain the situation. My father is Luther Martin Riggs. He is, or was, the lead preacher at the First Baptist Church of Christ."

"Aren't they the fuckers that protest the soldiers' funerals, and say that the outbreak occurred because God is punishing us?" Ackmed and Kevin give me puzzled looks at this revelation. "What, I watch the news for the news, not the anchors. They also have a website."

"Designed by me. My father made me do it. In addition to protesting dead soldiers' funerals, they also hate gay people and anyone who isn't white. They believe that all lower races were designed to be slaves to the white man, because slavery is in the bible."

"So is incest, do they believe in that too?" Ackmed has no tolerance for intolerance, unless that intolerance is directed at zombies.

Matt seems surprised that Ackmed has read the Christian bible. "No, it's pretty much just the slave thing."

After a second or two, Matt looks up. "We were ready for this whole zombie thing from the get go. My father believed that the end of the world was coming, and had stocked our church with plenty of canned goods, guns, and ammunition.   When the outbreak was first reported, he called every Church member in the Midwest area to our compound here in Chicago. About 500 devout followers showed up. My father thanked them for coming, and told them that the zombies were here to help end the world. He went on to say that the only way we could prevent the end was to eliminate all the sin that we saw around us."

"Let me guess, he started killing people for God." I am the writer, and also the strategist, so I can see where he was going with this.

"Not at first. At first, we just began fortifying the church. We had weapons, ammo, and food. We survived the initial outbreak with minimal losses. We even were bold enough to try to send out raiding parties."

"I thought you were doing well. What did you need to raid?" Kevin folds his arms over his chest and leans forward.

"Souls. Any survivors we found would be scared, hungry, and desperate. Their world had been turned upside down."

"And your father would be there to help them right it." Ackmed is a Muslim by birth, but hates organized religion. Putting a sharp edge in his voice, he asks, "And what about you, Matt? How many lost souls did you gather?"

Matt looks down and begins to talk softly. "It wasn't like they had anything else going for them." When no one answers, he looks up.

His voice rises to almost a desperate scream. "They were dying. Most of them were trapped. Their only hope was to join the church."

"Desperation and pain make for a lot of conversions?"

"Not as many as you might think. People remember the funeral thing. Some people even shot at us. Anyway, we didn't send out too many parties before one disappeared. We found them a couple of days later hanging from power lines. They had been lynched."

"Good," Ackmed replies with conviction.

Matt stares into space, and it is obvious that whatever he is seeing is not in the basement. "My brother was with them."

Even Ackmed is not cold enough to answer. Kevin sits back in his seat. "Bummer."

"That's why you should fear King Thaddeus." Matt stares at us again, daring us to refute his claim, but we remain silent.

"Who is he?" I ask, before the silence can go on for too long.

"We get scattered reports from people we find, and from his followers that we manage to capture, but we are not sure. As far as we can tell, he is a gang leader who united several of the gangs east of here after the zombies came. He feels about white people the way my dad feels about blacks."

We all take that in. Living in good old sheltered Lemont, we really didn't have many people who weren't white. This level of racism is pretty foreign to all of us, especially in light of the crazy state of the world.

"So, how do you feel about Thaddeus?" Kevin sits back on the recliner and folds his hands.

"I don't like him. Not because he is black, or anything." Matt glances at Ackmed self consciously. "My big brother, John, was the one who first taught me what bullshit my father was spouting. He helped me become someone other than my father. And now he's dead, killed by the same intolerance he fought against."

Matt sighs, seeming to shrink. "I am sick of all this hatred from everyone. I'm done."

He looks up, and seems to grow taller again. "I want to join you guys. I have no idea what you're doing here, but I've seen the internet; you guys know how to stay alive."

I glance at Kevin and Ackmed, trying to gauge their reactions. Kevin's broad smile gives his opinion away. Ackmed looks suspicious of this former white supremacist. I speak before anyone else. "Well, we will have to check some of your references, but we should be able to come up with something commensurate with your current salary."

Kevin smiles, but Ackmed stares at me like I just fucked his mom. Ackmed has never liked change anyway, and has always been slow to trust newcomers to our group, even when we were in high school. He was the one that first raised the idea that Hester might be a guy. In the end though, I am the writer, so I get to add the characters into the story.

"I'm glad you said that. Now I won't really have to shoot you." Matt puts the rifle down.

TWELVE

"Matt sounds like a very interesting person. I can't wait to meet him." Sam sits back in her chair, revealing cute bare feet. Her heels sit under the table. I can see up to the middle of her middle of her thigh, which makes her an interesting person in my view.

I don't really know how to answer questions about Matt, so I ignore her. "Are you bored or something?"

"No, I just like to sit like this. If I close my eyes, it helps me imagine the characters better. It's kind of like watching a movie in my head, just like when I read. So tell me more about Matt."

"Ok. Well, he was actually 15, not 16. His voice didn't crack or anything, but sometimes he would revert back to being a kid. Physically, he was blonde, and in decent shape. The zombie apocalypse had hardened him."

I feel a bit of jealousy surge through me because Sam's eyebrow rose up in the universal sign for, 'I'm interested,' when I talked about how in shape Matt was. I continue to describe Matt as best I can, avoiding dimples or blue eyes. She listens, eyes closed, as I tell her about the time that Matt killed four zombies with one swing of his sword. I tell her what a great shot he was with his rifle. Crazy conservative upbringing has its benefits, and firearm proficiency must be one of them. I don't want to give away any spoilers, so I summarize Matt as great guy that saved my life several times.

"You look very sad. Did something happen to Matt?" Sam always seemed to want to jump ahead. That drive for instant gratification makes her another good choice for marriage.

"Well, listen to the rest of the story, and you will find out."

■■

The grass is cool on my belly. I wish that my shirt didn't keep riding up as I crawl, but there is nothing to be done about it. I will just have to deal with the grass in the backyard and hope that there isn't anything waiting in the alley. It is so dark that I can't see what I am crawling over, so there is no way to avoid any glass or rocks. The crawling makes my legs burn and my arms feel like jelly.

And soldiers make it look so easy.

Crawling in the cold at night sucks, but it is the best way to get far from the house across the street that contains the men who want to shoot us. Matt had told us before we parted ways that the house was always garrisoned as some kind of outpost, so we needed to be careful and keep a low profile as we snuck out.

My stomach complains as rocks from the alley dig into my soft flesh, and Kevin exclaims, "Damn, these rocks are sharp."

Ackmed tells him to shut the fuck up, which he does until we crawl into the grass backyard of another house. "I just crawled through dog shit," Kevin complains, rolling onto his side. Ackmed and I both laugh, but tell Kevin to keep going. We are on a schedule and have to meet Matt soon.

"If he gets to us." Ackmed wipes sweat from his forehead. "This plan all depends on him getting to us."

A pessimist under the best of circumstances, Ackmed opposes this plan. He believes that Matt either can't pull it off, or that he will betray us to his psychotic father.

There isn't much to say, because we had argued about this all afternoon as we waited for the horde outside the house to dissipate. Eventually, I used my powers of persuasion and writing skills to convince Ackmed to follow along. I am the story teller, but this plan is so full of holes that if I put it in a book, it would probably be criticized for being too unbelievable.

But being as we are crawling though the backyard of a dog owner from the south side of Chicago while hiding from zombies and racists, I think that the suspension of disbelief factor is pretty high in this story already.

We reach the edge of the first street, and my first executive decision. Should we crawl across the street, or run? Crawling is slower, but will keep us hidden better. Running will be faster and easier on my stomach, but it is loud.

Being the writer is hard sometimes.

I can see large blobs on either side of the street, which I take to be parked cars. A raccoon walks right past us, his nose twitching in nervous excitement as he searches for food. Nothing else on the street moves, but my visibility is reduced by the darkness. Sighing, I decide that even if it means getting shot or eaten, I am done crawling. I jump to my feet. "Let's risk it."

The three of us begin to sprint, scaring the raccoon, who chastises us by chattering loudly as he disappears into the night. We run for almost three blocks, until we stop in front of a dark three story house. I throw myself to the ground and lay there, enjoying the cool grass on my stomach and face. My lungs hurt and my legs, which hurt before, protest the exertion. My heart is beating so loudly that I think it will give us away, and there is a stitch in my side. I start to cough, but silence it quickly. Vomit forces itself into my mouth, but I swallow with supreme effort and keep it down.

If I survive this, I need to start working out. At the very least, I need to do lots of cardio.

The first part of the plan has succeeded; we are sitting in front of what I hope is the correct house. That house, which had been used a couple of weeks ago by one of the reverend's scavenging teams, should be free of zombies. It is the perfect place to take shelter from a zombie attack, which is why we crawl two houses north to peer through the darkness at a second two story house.

"I hope you know what you're doing." Ackmed is almost growling as I raise my rifle in the air.

"Me too." I fire the gun four times.

The night has been far from silent. The wind howls and blows leaves down the street. Nearby animals, like our friend the raccoon, move through the night, unconcerned with humans or our problems. Our own terrified hearts beat loudly in our ears, and my brain constantly screams at me to turn around and go home where it is safe.

The rifle's report drowns out all of these things, temporarily deafening us. Even though I expect the noise, I still jump as it shatters the seemingly calm evening.

"Well, that's it. We're public enemy number one now." Kevin glances around and laughs, even though his comment is not funny.

Instead of being overwhelmed by the undead, nothing happens. The night's relative silence resumes as we sit on the lawn. It's kind of a letdown.

"Do you think it worked?" Kevin stands up and begins to pace, asking questions that none of us know the answer to.

"If we stick around here much longer, you can ask them." Ackmed stands and stretches. "We have our own problems to worry about now." Swinging his baseball bat menacingly, he disappears into the house behind us.

Kevin and I have no choice but to follow him into the darkness.

■■■

The house is empty. It has been trashed before us, and the window in the front room appears broken. Dark and unfamiliar shapes, which I take to be furniture that has been turned over, litter the living room and kitchen. Papers on the floor crunch as we walk on them.

After making sure that there are no zombies, we gather in the master bedroom upstairs. A king size bed full of crumpled clothing dominates the room, and several dressers sit at awkward angles. Jewelry and coins lay on the floor of the room, but they don't matter. What draws us into the master bedroom is the giant window facing the street.

As Ackmed opens the window a crack, the cold November night air seeps into the room. The familiar sounds of the night drift in as well; a bird chirps, a leaf blows, and a dog barks. Appearing satisfied, Ackmed sits back down. "Ok everyone, get down. We should be able to hear everything now."

This is the part of the plan that is really risky. The noise of the gunfire should have attracted zombies, and if there are any people outside, they should be fleeing from that horde. With luck, those people will be part of a team that Matt is on. With even more luck, he can slip away from the rest of the patrol in the confusion and make his way into our house without being spotted.

I don't even dare to hope that he can bring some of our equipment from the truck.

Nothing happens right away. Despite the window being open, it is still warmer inside the house than outside, so we take off our sweat soaked jackets and sit under the window. I tease Kevin about smelling like dog shit. Still nothing happens outside the window. Ackmed describes the crawlspace that we will hide in during phase three of our plan; it is packed with boxes, which is a good sign. And still nothing moves outside. Eventually, we lapse into a nervous silence. As a writer, I have an overactive imagination, so I fill this silent time thinking of all the things that can go wrong. Matt might have been denied permission to go out on patrol tonight. He might have grown too afraid of leaving the safety of the compound to join us. Barring that, the horde of zombies might have swallowed up Matt and his group before they could reach the houses.

I try not to think about the last possibility; that Ackmed was right, and Matt has betrayed us to his father.

Then, we hear the wonderful sound of boots hitting pavement outside. Footsteps, beautiful footsteps, running towards us in the dark.

"Where is it? Where is the fucking house?" A voice near panic is screaming outside. He sounds young and out of breath. "They are right behind us."

Matt's voice, calm and measured, comes next. "Calm down Kerry. It's just up the block. Slow down so we don't miss it."

The sound of boots slows as they approach our house. Kerry speaks again, and this time his voice loud, like he is standing right under the window. "What do you think happened? Do you think a band of the niggers got hit? Do we have any other patrols out?"

No one answers, but I hear Matt say, "Ok, the house is just up the block on the left. I am going to stay here to cover us and look for stragglers. Go to that house and wait for my instructions."

"I am staying with you brother. I am not leaving you alone here." The new voice is strong and confident. Whoever this is doesn't ask permission to stay with Matt; rather, he tells Matt what he is going to do. The voice is not angry or mean, however. It speaks to Matt with caring and concern, like a family member.

As the sound of boots fades away, Kevin whispers, "I thought Matt's brother was dead."

"It's a figure of speech." Ackmed makes a fist with his hands as I speak. I know that he wants to hit Kevin for risking our position.

"I thought only black guys talked like that, and they hate-" I put my finger to my lips just as Ackmed punches Kevin's leg. Kevin glares at Ackmed but doesn't speak any more.

"You don't have to stay, Brian. I'll be ok." Matt's voice breaks a bit. Hopefully Brian will think it is because Matt is nervous of the zombies.

"I couldn't live with myself if anything happened to you, Matt. Who would I talk to?"

Shit. Matt has a friend, and an extremely loyal one at that. It is going to be difficult for him to slip away unnoticed. Ackmed whispers, "Do you think I should shoot him when it starts?"

"Shoot him?" Kevin's sits up quickly, and his voice is loud with surprise. Ackmed raises his fist and I shush Kevin again. He indignantly sinks back down. "What, he gets to talk, but I don't?"

When he is seated, Kevin leans forward and whispers. "You're going to shoot an innocent man trying to help save his friend? What the fuck is wrong with you, Ackmed? We aren't murderers."

I wish that I could share in Kevin's moral outrage, but I had considered shooting him too. I just didn't have the balls to ask, for fear that I would have to do it. Relief washes over me; now that Ackmed has suggested shooting the man, it is his responsibility. My hands can remain clean. I don't want to shoot anyone.

Despite all that, though, I am the leader of the group. I can't just sit by and let Ackmed commit murder. It would be poor leadership, and downright unwriter like. I sigh and pick up my rifle. "I'll do it."

"Are you crazy, Malcolm? You can't just shoot people." I wish that Kevin would just shut up. It is going to be hard enough to pull the trigger without a moral compass talking me out of it.

"Look, if Matt doesn't get to us, we are trapped in the middle of zombie Chicago without any supplies. Just for good measure, there are white supremacists and black panthers thrown into the mix. We need him to help us. Besides, he is our friend now, we can't leave him here." I am surprised to hear Ackmed making such an impassioned speech, especially since he doesn't trust Matt.

"Well, that's true. But still, murder is a big step."

"Well, anything for a friend, right?"

"I guess, if there is no other choice." Kevin sounds defeated and upset.

That clever bastard. Ackmed has just gotten Kevin to agree to murder. And I thought that I was good at manipulating people.

Matt saves us by giving Brian instructions. "Look when they get here, fall back to the house. I will cover you until you get there. Then you can cover me. Ok?"

"You sure that you don't want to go first?"

"I run faster than you, old man." Matt laughs. I can't tell how old Brian is, but I would guess mid twenties from the sound of his voice. Ancient compared to Matt.

"Ok, but you are right behind me Matt." Brian is serious. The night is silent for a second, then gunfire erupts.

Through the noise, I hear Matt scream, "Go." The firing slacks off a bit as Brian stops firing and begins to run. After a couple of seconds, Brian screams at Matt, who doesn't answer.

"Matt, get your ass back here now. They are right on top of you."

I risk a peek out the window. Outside, Matt is firing into the nearest zombies, which are about five feet away from him. He turns and runs a few feet before falling down on the lawn.

. "Shit." Matt's voice is tinged with pain. "I can walk Brian. I only sprained it. Get in the house, I will be right inside."

"I'm not leaving you."

"Get inside Brian or I'll shoot you." Matt fires down the block. "The next one will hit you. I will go around the back door. Go open it for me, now."

Matt fires a couple of times at the approaching zombies and then sprints to the front door of our house. The door slams shut and we run downstairs. Matt is slumped down in front of the door, panting heavily. Tears run down his cheeks.

Kevin kneels next to Matt and puts his hand on his arm. "Are you ok?"

Matt shakes Kevin off and stands up. He sniffles and wipes his nose on his sleeve. "No, but I didn't get bitten."

I sense that he doesn't want to talk anymore, and we don't have time anyway.   "Great. Ackmed found a good hiding spot for us in the basement. I think it would be a smart idea to get down there as quickly as possible. "

THIRTEEN

It might not be ideal to live in, but it is an ideal hiding spot. About two feet tall and filled with boxes, the crawlspace is dark. Standing outside of it, I can't see the opposite wall 20 feet away for the darkness. Working silently, we move boxes for nearly forty five minutes. The boxes are all labeled with black marker. They say things like 'Sean's baby clothes,' and 'Army uniforms.' I try not to think of the lost lives that these boxes represent, or the fact that Sean is likely zombie food now; instead, I concentrate on avoiding the boxes labeled 'old books,' because they are heavy.

It is some of the most difficult work that I have ever done. Because the crawlspace is so small, we are forced to do all the work from our knees. All jokes about blowjobs aside, working on one's knees is very difficult. When added to the darkness, it causes chaos. Ackmed, the tall good looking star of our movies, keeps hitting his head on the ceiling. Spider webs stick to Kevin's beard. My knees scream from kneeling on the rough floor and my legs began to shake. My back aches, and I want to sleep.

If I survive, I really need to start working out. Maybe I will get a Kinect or something.

It is all worth it when I finally lean my head against the back wall of the crawlspace and stretch out. Peering through the darkness, I can only see the vague outlines of boxes. Safe from discovery behind our musty fortification, I stretch out. My arms and legs feel warm and hard as they contract with blood flow.

We lay there for a long time, each lost in our own thoughts. I find myself drifting into that wonderful arena of half sleep, where fantasy and reality combine to form vivid adventures.

Hester Prynne, or at least what I hope Hester Prynne looks like, is grating her hips back and forth in a circle. The rocks of the crawlspace dig into the backs of my legs, but I don't care. The pleasurable sensations on the front of my body far outweigh any discomfort that I am feeling elsewhere. Before I can offer to take her out of the crawlspace, she leans her face close to mine. I feel her smooth hair with my hand. She smells like apple cinnamon. Her lips part and we lean closer together. I want to taste her, to drink in the smell of her perfume.

Hester leans back just as we are about to kiss. Giving me a coy smile, she says in a surprisingly deep voice, "Well that went well."

"You finished already?" I smile back at Hester, pleased at how good I have become at sex. Killing zombies must agree with me.

"Finished with what Malcolm?" Hester disappears, and I am left staring at Kevin's bearded face. "I just was saying that I think that the plan is going well."

Sitting up so quickly that I hit my head on the ceiling, I realize where I am. Hester has gone far away into that netherworld of dreams, and I am sitting in a dark crawlspace with three other dudes. My muscles are sore and my dick is at half mast. The rocks still dig into the back of my legs, but without Hester as a distraction, the pain is much more noticeable.

I need to get laid, if only for my own sanity.

Thud Thud. The ceiling above our heads begins to shake as heavy footfalls land on the floor above. "Matt? Where are you, bro?" Brian's voice echoes throughout the house as Matt sits bolt upright.

Thud Thud. The noises get softer but more frequent as Brian runs upstairs. I barely hear a soft, defeated, "Matt, are you up here, man?" Matt sits forward on his knees, as if he is ready to pounce.

Thud Thud. The footsteps are again over our heads. The ceiling shakes. "Brian, he isn't here. Let's get the fuck home." It's Kerry, self assured now that there is no danger.

Thump. The ceiling shakes harder as Brian stamps his foot on the ground. "You don't know that. He might be downstairs."

Thud Thud. Quick footsteps move across the floor, then a third voice, empathetic and reminding me oddly of Kevin joins the conversation. "Of course, Brian. Let's check down there. Even if he isn't downstairs, he could have gotten away from the horde and be making his way back to the church. Maybe we will find him there."

Thud Thud. The steps are loud now, deafening. The men's voices are loud and close to us.

"See, nothing fucking here." Kerry swears a lot for a Christian.

"Wait. What about the crawlspace?"

I can see a small light as Brian shines his flashlight, the rays peeking through the sides of the boxes. I don't move. I try not to even think.

"Man, I told you, he isn't in there. Look at these boxes. They are heavy." We hear a thud as Kerry kicks the front of our fortification, causing a box near me to fall right on my foot, which protests this newest indignity with a sharp pain. With horror, I see that the box is labeled 'Science fiction books.' Robert Heinlein and Isaac Asimov wrote some long, heavy books. The bastards.

I try not to move. It doesn't hurt too badly, but it isn't comfortable. Kerry continues. "There is no way that he could have moved all these boxes alone. Besides, why would he hide in a crawlspace?"

Brian has no answer, but the soothing voice that sounds like Kevin does. "Brian, we can't stay here long. You know that the zombies or someone else will be back soon. We should get to the Church before it is light. There is always a chance that Matt made it back there."

Brian sniffles. "You fucking know he didn't."

"If that's the case, my friend, then I am truly sorry. We have all lost loved ones in this battle against evil, but we must go on. We must endure."

Thud Thud. The boots get softer now as the group goes back upstairs. I imagine Brian, his head hung in grief, slowly ascending the stairs.

Thud Thud. Slam. The front door opens and closes quickly. They are gone, again turning us into four dudes sitting alone in a dark crawlspace.

An hour later, we are all standing in the basement. I want to ask Matt how he is doing, but don't know how. He hasn't laughed at any of our jokes as we moved the boxes out of the way. Kevin attempts to reassure Matt, but he again waves him off. "Lets just get some sleep. I get the master bedroom."

Even though I am writing the story, I feel that Matt probably needs the extra space, so I don't fight him. I stumble upstairs into a room that has action heroes on the walls and a sports car shaped bed. This is way better than the master bedroom; I always wanted a car shaped bed.

I am hoping to at the very least make some engine noises, if not reenact an entire scene from Knight Rider, but the moment my body lands on that soft bed I begin to feel every ounce of my twenty five years. My back hurts, my legs hurt, and my arms hurt. Even my dick hurts a little. I must have scraped it against a rock or something while I was crawling around downstairs.

Before I can even so much as rub my sore dick, I begin to drift off to sleep. Hester again fills my thoughts, this time offering to make me feel all better. Just as she begins to examine my injured member, she looks up at me and asks sweetly, "Don't you want to have a night watch, Mal?"

None of my friends call me Mal. I tried to get them to start when Serenity came out, but it didn't take. I like the way it sounds on Hester's lips. Desperate for her to continue, I stroke her head. "No. Why would anyone bother us in this abandoned house?"

FOURTEEN

I don't really dream after that, which is kind of sad. I really want to find out what Hester was planning to do after I reassured her that we were safe in the house. Instead, I awaken to a poke to the stomach. Groaning, I push at whatever is poking me. "Go away, Ackmed. I am not in the mood for any jokes."

The poking continues, harder now. I open my eyes, cursing at Ackmed. When the world comes into focus, I see a bald black man standing over me with a shotgun.

The man smiles sweetly and asks, "Are we awake?"

I have to restrain myself from replying, "We are not sure. Are we black?" Mel Brooks may be an outdated reference, and I don't want to be taken for a racist if he doesn't get it. I only nod, hoping that I can find away to escape him.

"Good. Get up. Slowly." The sweetness in his voice has disappeared, replaced by a deep baritone that matches his gigantic frame. As I put on my jeans, I notice just how large this man is. At over six feet tall, the man is both fat and muscular at the same time. He must weigh over 350 pounds. Any thoughts of escape that I have quickly vanish as I stare at his arms, whose circumference rivals that of my thighs. His eyes sparkle with a dark intelligence. "Don't even think about it," he tells me.

There is no way that I can do anything but meekly go downstairs to the living room, where I find Kevin, Matt, and Ackmed all standing with similar looking black men. Each of them has their hands held above their heads.

"Let's go," our black man says, motioning to the door with his shotgun. "Malcolm, you take the sand nigger first. He looks the most dangerous." Ackmed draws his shoulders up, and looks almost proud at being called dangerous.

I can't resist. Besides, maybe a little humor will help the situation. "Where should I take him?"

No one else laughs, but one of the black men frowns and looks confused. He could be the mirror image of the man behind me, except that his eyes possess a certain kind of emptiness rather than intelligence.

The smaller man points at me. "His name is Malcolm too. The brown one is Ackmed, and the bearded one is Kevin."

When Malcolm still looks puzzled, the smaller man sighs. "Just go, like Michael said."

"Ok, J'Marcus." Malcolm grabs Ackmed by the arm and drags him out of the room.

Ackmed moves outside and mumbles, "At least they didn't think I was black."

"You're a fan?" Kevin regards J'Marcus curiously.

He nods. "Surely you don't think that we are all ignorant field hands."

"Where are you taking us?" I turn towards Michael, who is the large man that brought me downstairs. I had hoped that our history together would gain me some favor, but Michael doesn't respond.

"They are taking us to Thaddeus." Matt sounds depressed.

"But Thaddeus hates white people," Kevin adds, rather unnecessarily.

For an answer, the huge man smirks. "Fuck you fanatics." Indicating Kevin with a giant index finger, he tells J'Marcus and Kevin to leave and, "Go talk about <u>Star Wars</u> or something."

J'Marcus and Kevin depart, giggling at some unheard joke as they leave the house.

I try to tell the giant that we are not fanatics, but he interrupts me. "Shut up white boy. You ain't going to tell me no lies no more."

"How do you stay away from the zombies? Are you just going to feed us to the horde?" Matt sounds young and scared.

"Well, skinny white boy, someone finally asks me a question that deserves an answer. Here's your answer. Don't you worry your skinny white head about it. We got a way. And you bout to find out that way. " Michael nods to the last man, whom he calls Kemwebay, and tells him to go.

"I'm not going anywhere until you tell me how." Matt seems to be more afraid of the zombies than of Kemwebay. This proves to be a mistake, because Kemwebay walks up to Matt and somewhat casually slaps him across the face. He falls to the ground and looks up, shaking his head back and forth as if to clear it.

Kemwebay, with no apparent effort, lifts Matt to his feet. Scoffing him playfully on the head, Kemwebay says, "Just know you be safe as long as you listen." Matt is smart enough not to say anything else, and they walk out the door.

"Alone at last," I say to Michael, who ignores me.

"Let's get outside. I gonna show you a whole new way to travel."

We walk outside. By day, the street looks much less terrifying. Dead zombies litter the street from last night's firefight, but other than the occasional body, it could be any normal day in Chicago. Cars are parked and squirrels run up and down trees. A light mist falls from the sky, making the already cold November morning seem even colder.

I begin to walk towards the street, but a huge hand on my shoulder stops me. "We not going that way. We going this way." Pointing at the house next to us, Michael gives me a grin. "Look up."

Standing on the roof next door staring at me are Kevin and J'Marcus. Kevin waves.

■■

Once I'm on the roof, I don't have time to admire the view. That's ok; it consists of some leafless trees and brick houses. The real sight on the roof is the people. Kevin and J'Marcus are standing alone, whispering quietly and giggling. Kemwebay and Matt each have hold of one of Ackmed's arms. Ackmed has turned paper white, which is quite a feat for someone of his complexion. He is sweating in the morning cool and jerking his head to the left and right.

"What's wrong with him?" I point at Ackmed.

J'Marcus answers through giggles. "He's afraid of heights."

"Malcolm." Ackmed's voice is coming in gasps. He can't finish the sentence, so he just says my name and then stares at me with pleading eyes.

"What?" Large Black Malcolm looks confused. "Should I shoot him?"

J'Marcus sounds tired. "His name is Malcolm, too."

Ackmed finds his breath. "Malcolm, get me off this fucking roof."

Kevin and J'Marcus giggle again. I sense an unhealthy friendship developing between the two. Hopefully, the target of their sarcasm will remain Ackmed.

"Hey white boy." Michael sounds calm and somewhat amused.

"I'm not white asshole. I'm Indian and Middle Eastern." Ackmed can only form one word sentences as he stares down at the ground, so he pauses for a full second after each word.

"Just be cool man. I will fix it." I try to sound confident, but even though I am the writer, I have no idea how I can write Ackmed off this roof.

"I'll fix it." Michael pushes past me and stands next to Ackmed. Shifting his shotgun, he places the cold steel directly under Ackmed's chin. Kevin and J'Marcus stop laughing.

Bending down so that his face is directly next to Ackmed's, Michael tells him to stop struggling. Then, he cocks the shotgun. "I'm only going to say this once, so pay attention. Stop fighting, and chill the fuck out. You might be thinking that falling gonna hurt, and you be right. But no one's ever fallen off one of these roofs in all the time we been doing this."

He pauses dramatically, then taps his shotgun. "This shotgun, however, killed many people. So if I was you, I would think about what's scarier, the ground or the shotgun."

For a moment, I think that Ackmed is going to retort, but he straightens up. "Alright, what's next?"

Michael motions to the edge of the roof, which causes Ackmed to blanch again. "Get the ladder."

■■

"Michael was right when he told me that they had a new way to travel."

Sam watches me intently, and I think for a second that I could get lost in her brown eyes. She twitches with anticipation, so I let her have some satisfaction by telling her how we placed ladders between the buildings of the city and crawled across them, without the zombies even knowing that we were above them.

"That's ingenious. She slaps me on the arm and smiles. "And so simple, too."

"The only problems were the corners. There was no way a twenty foot ladder could reach across an entire intersection, so when we reached one, Michael picked two volunteers-

"Did you just use air quotes with me when you said volunteers?" Sam frowns and sounds mockingly angry. "I hate air quotes."

"I did use air quotes, but with good reason. The volunteers-"

"Stop doing that." Sam moves her arm away, so I stop making air quotes and continue.

"The volunteers had to descend the ladder first. Once they were on the ground, they needed to clear a house of zombies. That way, if we were attacked, we would have a place to go and wait out the horde. Only then did we go down the ladder in groups of two, just like when we left the safe house."

"Sounds complicated."

"It wasn't all that bad. I had to go with Michael at the first intersection. Then Kevin and J'Marcus went. We didn't see any zombies until the time Michael pointed at Kemwebay and Matt."

■■

"Kemwebay and smart white boy. " Michael still hasn't bothered to learn our names, which I find both offensive and unsettling.

"Wait." Matt holds his hand out like a crossing guard telling car to stop.

"Malcolm, throw him off the roof." Michael sounds casual, like he has just asked Malcolm to take out the trash. He points at me. "Other Malcolm, you go with Kemwebay."

Black Malcolm shrugs and starts walking towards Matt. Kevin and J'Marcus begin to furiously protest, their voices rising to panicked screams. They only shut up when Michael tells them, "I will throw anyone off the roof who attracts attention to us. That includes brothers, J'Marcus."

J'Marcus and Kevin stop talking, but Matt begins to whisper so loud that it sounds like a tiny shout. "Wait, I am not saying that I won't go. But I need some kind of protection. What good am I to Kemwebay without a weapon?"

Malcolm reaches Matt and draws his gigantic arms back. "Malcolm, wait a second. He's right."

Malcolm looks momentarily disappointed, but his face soon resumes its normal blank stare.

"Great. Thanks. I'll just take my rifle from Malcolm, and we will go." Matt holds his hands out towards the hulk in front of him. "It's the one that says Bad Mother Fucker on it."

Everyone but Michael and Malcolm laughs at the <u>Pulp Fiction</u> reference. "Ain't no way I'm giving some white fanatic a gun." Malcolm surveys the street, and then points at a corpse laying half a block up. Most of the body has been devoured, leaving only bones and a tattered blue shirt, but next to these remains, a baseball bat rests against the curb. "When you guys get down, run and get the bat while Kemwebay covers you."

"A fucking baseball bat? What good will that do me?" Like most 15 year olds, Matt seems to have a short memory- it seems that he has already forgotten Malcolm preparing to throw him off the roof.

This time, Michael doesn't send Malcolm. He grabs Matt by the front of his shirt and lifts him up so that they are at eye level. "You keep arguing and making noise, you gonna be using your fists. Got it? Now go get that fucking baseball bat, and clear that house."

Michael sounds oddly like a drill instructor.

Dropping Matt onto the roof, he tells Kemwebay, "If he gives you any trouble, shoot the fucker."

Kemwebay looks cheered by the thought, and Malcolm looks a bit jealous.

FIFTEEN

Matt retrieves the bat without incident, and then he and Kemwebay disappear.

I stand and stare at the house. It has the same basic architecture as all the other south side homes in the area; brick exterior, with four or five concrete steps leading to a spacious front porch. This particular house has flower pots on its porch with shriveled white flowers inside. I am not watching the house for the architecture or the horticulture, though. I am intently studying the exterior, as if that will give me any idea as to what is going on inside. Even though Matt is new to our group, he is one of my characters. I am responsible for his development, and I don't want that development to be stopped short by a zombie.

Michael stands next to me, also staring at the house in vain. Kemwebay is his character, just as Matt is mine. "How good is your boy?"

I shrug. "To be honest, I am not really sure."

Michael takes his eyes off the house just long enough to show me an expression of contempt. "You're not sure of your own man?"

I laugh as I realize how insane it sounds. "I just met him yesterday. He seems good though, very good."

"You trust him?"

I think about Matt pretending to sprain his ankle the night before. "Yeah, I do."

"Kemwebay's a bad motherfucker. If shit goes down with the freaks, he's the best I got. If shit goes down with your boy, he 's gonna whoop his ass." I can't tell if Michael is trying to threaten me or simply reassure himself.

There seems to be no answer for that, so I go back to looking at the house. Hours seem to pass, and then a pistol shot breaks through the morning calm. Another shot follows a couple of seconds later. I look at Michael, who appears ready to leap over the side of the building. Matt comes sprinting to the porch. He has no more concern for noise discipline after the shots, so he just screams at us. "Get the fuck down here, now."

With that, he goes back inside. Michael is moving from the moment Matt appears. A huge black blur, he is already down the ladder and on the ground by the time Matt is back inside. I follow as quickly as I can.

The house opens to a linoleum mudroom and hallway that extends straight ahead to the kitchen. On my right is the carpeted living room, complete with a fire place and love seat. Pictures dot the room; a photo of a young blonde man wearing a tuxedo and an even younger blonde woman dressed in white holding hands, that same blonde man clinging to a newborn pink bundle, and an older couple, who I presume to be the proud grandparents. All stare at me with bright ignorant smiles as I enter the house.

A dead woman stares up at me, her blue eyes open. She's laying on her back, her long blonde hair streaked with blood, framing her face with a crimson gold. She lies with her petite waist right on the golden divider, which separates the carpeted front room and the linoleum hallway.

Inside the front room, Matt stands, holding his pistol while Michael kneels, whispering something. Lying between them and bleeding onto the cream colored carpeting is Kemwebay. He look surprised to be lying on the carpet with his neck torn half open.

"A zombie jumped us in the hallway," Matt explains to Michael, gesturing toward the blond woman on the ground with his pistol. "She came out of nowhere. We thought the house was clear. He couldn't dodge it. After he went down, I took care of her with his pistol. I'm sorry."

Matt hangs his head. Kemwebay opens his mouth as if to speak, but nothing comes out. Little bubbles form in his ruined neck as he fights to breathe. Michael begins to weep, and lowers his head and begins to shake. I can't see his face, but it looks like he is crying. Between sobs, he says," Kemwebay, I'm so sorry."

Michael looks up, and I draw back, expecting the inevitable anger that accompanies grief. But there is none of that now, only a radiating sadness around Michael that makes his huge form appear almost childlike. "I-Kemwebay and I promised that we wouldn't allow each other to turn into one of them."

Matt nods solemnly, and raises his pistol. It occurs to me that he could shoot Michael now, while he is vulnerable. J'Marcus is practically on our side anyway, and we can easily outwit Black Malcolm.

Michael picks up Kemwebay's huge hand and cradles it next to his face. "Kemwebay, I am so very sorry," he says again. Matt places the pistol on Kemwebay's forehead and fires. The noise makes me jump. Michael sniffles for a second, then breathes deeply a couple of times.

He stands up and looks Matt in the eyes. Holding out a hand to Matt, he glances again at Kemwebay. "Thank you. He is-was my brother. I couldn't-"

Matt shakes Michael's hand, then bends down and gently closes Kemwebay's now unseeing eyes. He places his tiny white hand onto Michael's giant shoulder. "I understand. I have a friend like that too."

I think guiltily of Brian being dragged from the crawlspace last night by his companions as the others file into the house. Surveying the scene, Malcolm finds some of the anger that Michael had not. Rage closing in on his face, he points his shotgun at Matt. "That mother fucker shot Kemwebay."

"Stop it," Michael interrupts, gesturing at Matt with his free hand. "He is a good man."

Malcolm's face resumes its normal confused look and he lowers his shotgun. Michael kneels again and holds Kemwebay's hand. Gently, Matt touches his shoulder again. As if speaking to a child, Matt says, "Michael, we need to go into the basement now.

Michael shuffles into the basement as if he himself has become a zombie, and we follow.

• •

The basement is unfinished, but whoever owned the house must have been a card player, because an honest to God poker table sits on one end of the room. The three black men, Malcolm, J'Marcus, and Michael all huddle around it. They talk softly amongst themselves, sometimes staring into space, sometimes laughing, sometimes crying, and the whole time grieving.

The four of us sit clustered around a computer desk on the far side of the room. J'Marcus had given Kevin his camera back sometime that day, and he spent much of the time fighting with an ancient Windows 98 machine to upload photos.

Ackmed looks at me, then at Matt. "Malcolm, I'm sorry that I fought you about Matt coming."

"It's alright. I am used to you being an asshole and then apologizing. Usually in a stranger's basement."

"Fuck you."

It seems like I am back in control of the story, which is good, because I don't like the plot twists that Ackmed has created. Being captured by black militants with stereotypical names like Kemwebay and J'Marcus sounds kind of predictable.

Matt listens to our banter and appears confused, but doesn't inquire. I hadn't mentioned Ackmed's anger. It was clear that Ackmed didn't want Matt with, but I felt that even here, in the zombie apocalypse, there should be some kind of decorum. Thus it surprises me when Ackmed turns to Matt with the same serious face that he had just shown me. "I owe you an apology too. I am glad that you are with us."

Matt looks sheepish. "Thanks, but I have to go."

"Goddamn Windows 98 fucking piece of shit." Kevin slaps the side of the computer monitor, which has a blue screen now.

Matt looks concerned, but I ignore Kevin. "Why do you have to leave?"

Matt points at Kevin. "Is he going to be ok? What's wrong with him?"

Ackmed shakes his head. "It's before your time. Bill Gates used to be a fucking moron. Now what's this about you leaving? I just got all tender and shit."

Matt looks down. I can tell that this is his first breakup. "Look, I really like you guys, but seeing Kemwebay go down like that really made me think of Brian. He's my best friend, and now he is all alone."

"So you found someone else?" Kevin's computer is slowly rebooting.

"It's not us, it's you." Ackmed looks mock sad, pretending to cry.

Kevin strokes his beard, like a philosopher. "Before you run out of our lives and break our hearts, let me ask you this. Why didn't you just ask him to come with us the first place? Everyone is welcome here."

"Unless you ask Ackmed," Matt responds, pointing at Ackmed as if in judgment. "Seriously, though, Brian has a wife back at the compound. She's pregnant, and he wants to keep them safe. He would never have left without her. I'm the only one that knows that they aren't true believers."

"So you joined our group just to tell us you couldn't join our group. This is confusing." We all giggle at Ackmed's comment. Then, he turns serious for the second time in just a few minutes. "What if we got Brian and his wife back? Would all of you come with us?"

I can't believe my ears. This is the same Ackmed that was so upset when I allowed Matt to join our group that he threatened to leave at one point. He wanted to write a different story, with only three protagonists. But now, a mere twenty four hours later, he is not only inviting Matt to join the group, but volunteering us for yet another hair brained rescue operation. I have been back in control of the story for moments, and already major character development has occurred. God, I am good.

Matt looks surprised too. He must have been expecting Ackmed to be a static character. Much like most of the agents that I have sent manuscripts to, he doubted my writing prowess as well.

"I suppose that they would be more than happy to leave, but the big problem would be getting them out. Brian will never leave without Susan, and women never leave the camp." Matt looks pained. "Besides, don't you guys have your own mission here? Wouldn't this get you off track in a big way?"

"Don't worry, Matt," I say without thinking. "Side plots are important to a novel." Shit. Did I just say that out loud?

Matt tilts his head to the side like a dog does when he is confused.

"Er- I mean, this is important, and the more the merrier, right? Do you think that Brian and Susan will help us rescue the First Lady?"

Matt thinks for a bit, then nods. "Of course. He's a Democrat."

"Got it. The videos are uploaded. Eat a dick Bill." We all look at Kevin, who appears to have missed the last part of our conversation. "So, what's our next move?"

"Same as it always was." Michael's booming voice sounds from right behind me. "We are taking you to meet Thaddeus."

SIXTEEN

"After all of that, Michael was still going to turn you over to Thaddeus?" Sam's voice has an edge to it.

"I was just as angry when I found out. But, looking at it from his perspective, he had no choice. Thaddeus was his king, and Michael was his vassal. His loyalty was still to Thaddeus, and we were still his prisoners."

"So nothing changed?"

"Not exactly. Michael was a lot nicer to us. Instead of calling us things like, "White boy," or "Cracker," he called us by our names. When he instructed us, we were given explanations. He was still in charge our our little group, but I was ok with that. This was his world now, not mine. We needed a guide anyway."

We sit in silence for a second before I continue. "What they did to that neighborhood was incredible. The area around Midway Airport contains mostly small homes and industrial parks. Some of the bigger streets have stores or restaurants, but the meat of the area is the homes. The six block radius around Midway Airport had been utterly transformed. There was a ladder between every building, and semi trucks were parked sideways across intersections. You could walk the entire way to the airport without ever touching the ground. They called it the Thaddeus Memorial Highway."

"Clever." Sam seems eager to attack the Black Panthers. Since they had done nothing in this story other than attack me, this makes me very happy. Sam is protective of me, which makes warmth again flood through my body. She isn't even touching me this time.

"Well, they weren't that great at names, but they were fantastic with architecture. You have to appreciate the conditions that they worked in to build up this network. Michael told us that his crew had lost nine of its twelve members building the highway, but Kemwebay was their first loss since it had been finished a month before. We were just asking what gang J'Marcus had been in when we came in sight of the airport...."

▪▪

J'Marcus seems amused, as does Michael. "Not me. I am not a stone cold type. I am just a graphic designer from Boston that got caught at Midway Airport waiting for a connection."

Before I can question him more, Kevin interrupts. "Would you be interested in doing some work for our website?"

He never answers us, because Michael urges us down off the truck trailer that we were walking on. "Let's not keep the man waiting. There's the base."

The base turns out to be Midway airport itself. It makes for a natural fortification; Homeland security had build giant ten foot concrete walls with barbed wire around the entire airport to keep out terrorists. They appear to keep out zombies just as well. A gate near us opens, and we run into the compound.

It no longer looks like an airport. The first thing I notice is a gigantic Mexican man manning the biggest gun that I have ever seen. Mounted on a tripod, the gun is at least six feet of polished metal. Even from a few feet away the barrel seems as large as my head. Beyond the man, I notice that the airfield looks like an army base. Sandbag positions bristling with more big guns are situated at every gate. Armed men, all black or Mexican, patrol the grounds in groups of three. They carry weapons as well, and walk with the alertness of professional soldiers.

With a loud crack, The Mexican cocks the machine gun and points it at us. I am in the lead, and the dark barrel of the gun is aligned directly with my face. The Mexican smiles venomously. "Welcome to Camp Thaddeus." His voice is surprisingly high.

Willing myself to turn away from the gun, I look for our guides, but Michael and the others have disappeared. There is a huge gray airplane hangar on my right. Deciding that they must have gone there to report in, I start to walk that way.

My path is immediately blocked by one of the patrolling groups that I had noticed earlier. Up close, the men are even more frightening. It is not their build; as a matter of fact, they are all thin and appear to be in their late teens. It is their eyes that frighten me. They look cold and soulless, similar to the eyes of the zombies. These youths have lived through a lot, and their dead and lifeless eyes tell a story of death and destruction.

I shiver as their leader, a black kid with a tattoo of a viper on his neck, points a pistol at me. "Where do you think you're wandering off to, White Devil?"

I want to reply, but suddenly my knees are weak and my throat is dry. This man would kill me without blinking. He would pull that trigger and lose no more sleep about it than I do when I kill NPC's in video games. He is more of an animal than a man now. Motioning to another airplane hanger, he tells me in a flat voice, "You going over there."

With no other choice, I walk towards the hanger, hoping that no one shoots me in the back.

▪▪

Once our captors slam the doors behind us, the bright morning turns instantly into a starless night. A huge dark shape stands out in the hanger. From what I can see, it looks like a helicopter. I can't tell what is on the other side of the hanger for the darkness, but an awful smell that reminds me of a portable toilet gives a hint as to what waits over there.

Ackmed stares at me. Even in the darkness, I can make out the glint of anger in his eyes. "Well this is just great."

Kevin tries to change the subject. "It stinks in here."

"Yeah, this whole trip stinks." Ackmed is still staring at me, and his eyes are cold.

If I were writing my character, I would have given Ackmed a witty retort and then challenge him with my gaze until he looked away. Ever the dominate male, I would then figure out an escape plan, rescue the President's wife, and fuck Hester until I collapsed from exhaustion.

But, I am not a character in a book; I am just plain old Malcolm Tushton. So instead of all those things, I look down and away as if studying the concrete floor.

Ackmed has no qualms about taking on the role of Alpha Male. He is, after all, our hero. "I'm talking to you Malcolm. This is a disaster. You have led us into a disaster. And it's only going to get worse. They're probably going to kill us, you know."

"They'll probably torture us first." I can't tell if Kevin is trying to lighten the mood, or is just too scared to realize what he is saying

I ignore Kevin. "Well what else could I have done, Ackmed? If you were in charge of this story, please, tell me what you would have done. Enlighten me, oh great leader."

"We wouldn't be here. You know why? Because if I were in charge, we would never have come into this shithole of a city, with its insane white people"- he points at Matt and then swings his arm at the door-"and even crazier black people. We would be safe by now, eating cheese curds from Culver's and planning a trip to LA. Instead, we are sitting in a shit hanger planning to be shot."

I can't believe that he is blaming me. I thought he had made such a development when he apologized earlier, but it seems that his rage has once again overcome his logic. With a shock, I realize that it is probably going to be like this the rest of the time we are stuck in the city. Ackmed will be happy to follow when things go well, but the minute things don't go as planned, he will want to be in charge. There will be no way I can ever win. If we hadn't come this way, and failed in our movie careers, Ackmed would have told me that it was my fault for not making us famous by rescuing the First Lady.

Suddenly very tired, I make my way to the other side of the hanger. "Fine, Ackmed, you want to be in charge, be in charge."

The other side of the hanger smells worse, but no one follows me. I sit in a relatively dry spot. Across the hanger, I hear Matt and Ackmed arguing. Their voices rise in anger, then they begin fighting, actually hitting each other. I don't move. I don't care anymore; it isn't my story to write, it's Ackmed's.

Kevin is screaming at me to get up and help him break up the fight, but I just close my eyes and think of Hester.

∎∎

Eventually, I move back towards the group. After a few hours, someone came over to pee, and then shit. Despite my anger at Ackmed, I don't want to sit near a pile of my friends' shit.

I sit apart from the group, which appears to have made up, because they sit brainstorming quietly. I can't make out all the details of the plot, but it sounds like Ackmed intends to fight his way out of the airport. I am not sure if I will be invited to join them, or if they will just leave me. Not that it matters very much anyway; stay or go, both are a death sentence.

The hanger, already uncomfortable with its darkness and concrete floors, now adds an all encompassing chill to its list of amenities. This cold is not a, "I'm in a movie theater and need a jacket," type of cold. This is cold in a way that made me forget what it is like to be warm. I lay shivering on the hard floor, comforted only by the fact that Ackmed must be as uncomfortable as I am.

I may be exaggerating a bit, but November nights in Chicago get pretty fucking cold.

I lay there on that freezing concrete for a long time. With no clock and nowhere to go, time takes on a whole new meaning. It is dark all the time, so there is no really good way to tell how much time has gone by. It seems like I have been sitting in the dark forever; hours or days could have passed.

My thoughts drift from Hester to Ackmed. Unlike Hester, Ackmed wears clothes in my thoughts. By my count, this makes the third time that Ackmed has tried to take over my story- once at Mr. Chimelski's, once when we were hiding from Matt's friends, and now.

The first time, I had taken control of the plot almost immediately, before any damage could be done. By the time Ackmed took over the second time, I had already agreed to help Matt; Ackmed was in charge, but he was still following my outline.

If he took over now, it would be his story and I would be a character in that story. I like being in control; that is why I like writing. When I write, I am in charge of the characters fates, their actions, and the setting. I don't like the idea of relegating myself to the role of mere observer. I would be like a reader, who can do nothing but hopelessly enjoy the pretty prose and wonder what will happen next.

That said, Ackmed has a point. I had written us into an almost impossible spot, one that may require a healthy dose of dues ex machina to get out of. Although none of my characters had died yet, we weren't exactly doing well. Maybe I should let him take over.

I could still add to the story. I didn't have to just read. Perhaps I could edit, or co-author. This could be a collaborative effort, provided my name was listed first on the cover.

And provided we lived.

My stomach begins to growl, leading me to believe that we had been sitting in the hanger for hours rather than days. The others began to stir as well, and mumble about food. I hurry to the shadow that looks like Ackmed. "We need to talk."

"You're right. We came up with a plan last night. Let me go pee first. Ackmed disappears to the other side of the hanger. He no longer sounds quite so angry.

The door bursts open, flooding the room with bright light and causing me to squint. Four men march in, all carrying guns. They look just as tough as the men that brought us into the hanger.

All the guns are pointed at us.

Ackmed appears out of the darkness, running at the men and screaming, "Now."

As if on command, Matt and Kevin begin to scream and charge the men. This apparently is Ackmed's grand plan. He really needs an editor.

The men wordlessly shoot Ackmed, who crumples to the floor and doesn't move. Turning towards Matt and Kevin, they fire again, stopping their mad charge.

Then, they turn to me, weapons raised. I try to raise my hands in surrender, but suddenly pain explodes in my stomach. I fall to the ground, striking the back of my head. I lay there looking at the ceiling and pondering life and death.

It doesn't hurt as much as I thought it would. My stomach hurts where the bullet struck me, but it feels more like a punch than anything else. A black face appears in front of me. My forehead explodes in pain, real pain, and as darkness closes around me, I know that I am dying.

SEVENTEEN

I wake up to darkness. My stomach and head still hurt.

I think at first that I must be dead. But, if I am dead, I would be in either Heaven or Hell. If Heaven is so great, I wouldn't be hurting at all. I also wouldn't have my hands tied behind my back. Conversely, if I were in Hell, I would be hurting much worse than I already am.

Concluding that I must not be dead, I further evaluate my situation. My biggest problem is that I can't see. My eyes don't hurt, so I must either have something over my face, or I have been frozen in carbonite. From the rough, itchy material on my face, I would guess that I had a burlap sack over my head. A cliché, to be sure, but I'm not the author anymore- Ackmed is.

Or at least Ackmed had been the author when he was alive. I remember Ackmed falling to the ground and not moving. Kevin and Matt had fallen as well. I am fairly certain from the pain that I have been shot in the stomach and the head. Why had I survived when the others had died?

The only conclusion that I can reach is that I must be immortal. But what kind of immortal? I can't feel any blood on my stomach; perhaps the wound is already healing. I might be like Wolverine. Maybe I am more like a low grade superman- I can be injured momentarily, but not permanently damaged. I think that I am looking forward to flying the most. Followed closely by using my xray vision to look at girls.

I am just wondering exactly how I will lift the Hammer of Doom when a familiar voice next to me begins screaming. "Take this fucking thing off my head and fight me like a man."

It is Ackmed. As he continues to scream obscenities, I hear Kevin talking as well. "I can't see. My chest really hurts."

All three of us had survived, which can only mean one thing. We are highlanders. How can I kill my best friends? On a cliff? I feel a wave of panic as I realize that I am not as good a swordsman as Ackmed, but I content myself with the thought that I at least have a kick ass theme song by Queen.

Without being able to control it, I start to hum *Princes of the Universe*. Strong hands lift me to my feet, and a powerful, confident voice tells me to shut up. "Walk," the voice continues. It sounds serious and uncompromising. I begin to walk, guided by the strong voice.

Although I stop humming, I still have *Princes of the Universe* stuck in my head.

■■

We walk for a long time. My head and stomach still throb, and my knees complain about my choice of sleeping arrangements. I snap and pop as I move. I am not sure how far we go because we walk up and down stairs several times. I begin to breathe heavily and quickly.

I really need to start working out.

Eventually, the voice tells me to stop. The burlap sack is removed from my head, and the light causes my eyes to hurt. Wherever I am, there are wooden floors, a mahogany bar with clean crystal glasses hanging over it, and sports memorabilia on the walls. Tables complete with tablecloths dot the room, each containing a full set of silverware and a folded napkin.

The front of the room is dominated by a black man sitting in a chair with a giant wooden back, like a throne. The black man is of average size and wearing round rim glasses. His pants are around his ankles, and kneeling in front of him is a topless woman, her head buried in his lap. She is white, and the paleness of her back stands out in sharp contrast to the dark brown of his skin.

One of our guards giggles, a sick and twisted sound. "That's King Thaddeus, getting himself some white pussy."

"It's good to be the king." Kevin's fondness for Mel Brooks rivals mine.

None of the men with us smile, but Thaddeus smiles and points to us, his arm extending over the woman's head as it bobs up and down. I guess Mel Brooks references are not outdated after all. Or he is smiling because he is getting blown by a beautiful woman?

Thaddeus's body shakes with orgasm. Wiping her mouth, the girl stands up and puts on her shirt. Without so much as a nod to the girl, Thaddeus pulls his pants up and advances towards us. It is indeed good to be the King. Dismissing the group that brought us with a nod, Thaddeus motions to a table. "Forgive me, but there was an urgent manner I had to attend to. Please, be seated."

For the first time, I notice the pair of guards flanking Thaddeus throne. Both hold rifles at the ready and are tall and muscular. Both regard us impassively. All they need are red cloaks and they could be members of the Emperor's personal body guard.

I had pictured Thaddeus as a huge man, thickly muscled and bald. Kind of like Ving Rhames, only with Ebonics. In my mind, Thaddeus was an intelligent man to be sure, but a vicious and primal one as well. He was a cross between a man and a beast, reaching back to a time when men led fur clothed nomads on expeditions to pillage.

The man standing before us looks quite normal. Of average height and build, nothing stands out about him. He even has a closely cropped head of hair. He speaks English better than I do, and his wire rim glasses give him an intelligent, if bookish look.

Turning to one of the guards he says, "If you please, Albert, bring our guests some sustenance." Turning toward us, he adds, "We have a pitiful number of Harry Carey's finest steaks left, so if I may again beg your pardon, portion sizes will be small this morning. I can assure you, though, that their quality is exquisite."

Thaddeus regards Ackmed. "That is, unless our Hindu friend here is unable to partake in beef?"

Ackmed shakes his head. "Actually, I'm a Muslim."

"Fascinating." Thaddeus sits down at the table and folds his hands. We sit as well. The chair is standard fair for a restaurant, but compared to the ground in the hanger, it feels wonderful. My back cries in relief. The room is warm, and I swear I hear soft piano music being played. This is as different from the warehouse as I can imagine.

Albert returns, carrying crystal wine glasses of water for us. Despite his bulk, he moves with an easy grace, and sets the glasses on the table without spilling a drop. I wonder if the Emperor's Royal Guard ever served meals.

"I figured that the hanger was needed to torture someone else. You must have captured some women or children that you can throw in there before you sodomize them, right?" Matt sounds bitter.

My stomach is growling and I need to eat. Kevin leans in towards Matt. "Dude, relax. He is going to serve us steak."

"Relax?" Matt stands up and points at Thaddeus. "He's going to kill us anyway, so what's the point of being so nice?"

Everyone begins talking at once. Ackmed immediately begins interrogating Thaddeus, while Kevin and I frantically attempt to get Matt to stop using racial slurs. Thaddeus shakes his head slowly and sadly. Albert raises his rifle into the air and fires one shot into the ceiling. Without a word, he points the gun squarely at Matt's chest. The other guard, forgotten until now, points a rifle at Ackmed. A laser pointer makes a mark in the center of Ackmed's forehead. Everyone stops talking and lapses into a silence that lasts a full thirty seconds.

When Thaddeus again speaks, he sounds less like a mild mannered college professor and more like the monarch that he proclaims to be. "Listen up. When I say King Thaddeus, I mean King, with a capital K. That means all of you treat me with respect. With a capital R. I hold all the power here."

Thaddeus looks at Matt, who has been rolling his eyes throughout his speech. "Let's get a few things straight. I don't kill people unless they try to kill me. I am not an animal or a monster. There are a succinct set of rules here, and I must obey them as well as Albert or William here." He indicates the guards.

Matt evidently has a suicide wish. "What rule says that you get to rape women?"

Thaddeus doesn't quite yell, but when he speaks, it is in a tone that makes him seem bigger. "I am going to give you a chance to listen while explain the way things work here. I don't have to explain anything to you, but I will if you listen. These interruptions are beginning to annoy me."

The unspoken threat hangs in the air like a bad odor. "Despite what you may have heard, we do not kill people out of turn in this organization. What we are, what this outbreak means to us, is a second chance for our people."

The words are out of my mouth before I realize what I am saying. "Your people?"

"My people as in the black man, the brown man, and the red man. Anyone that the government has given a raw deal to. This revolution is providing us with a chance to remedy that error. What we have created here is a nation for us, created by us. All of our people are welcome." Thaddeus pauses for a long time before looking at directly at Matt. "Now, you may ask me any questions that you wish, as long as you use a respectful tone."

"What about white people?" This time, Matt sounds more inquisitive than angry.

"White people are not welcome stay permanently with us, except in very specific circumstances. That said, we do not just kill the white people we find. We take them in until they completely recover. They are then taken into an area not under my rule and released. All people are welcome to return at any time to trade goods or information." Thaddeus sounds civilized and calm.

Some venom returns to Matt's voice. "So you don't murder them, the zombies do."

Thaddeus's retort comes quickly, as if he has had this argument before. "Just as you didn't murder black slaves, diseases and long hours in hot cotton fields did."

Kevin helpfully speaks up. "Matt never murdered any slaves. None of us have."

Thaddeus takes a sip of water. A drop escapes and runs down the corner of his mouth. He wipes it with a napkin and coughs. "You are correct. None of you actually murdered slaves, but the fact remains that your people have been effectively keeping my people in bondage, literal or physical, for well over four hundred years. The society that I have created here does not seek revenge for this barbaric act. We only seek seclusion. You think me barbaric? Let me point this out to you. While we do operate with segregation, as you did in the south, when a white person does not notice our black only sign, we do not lynch them. "

"Effective use of examples to prove your point." I can't help saying it. I have written several persuasive essays, and I recognize a well structured argument when I hear one. Furthermore, Thaddeus states his points eloquently. If he were a writer, then he would be a good one.

Ackmed glances at Matt and grins. "Another person that is all about tolerance."

"I support tolerance of all kind." Thaddeus sounds offended that the opposite could be implied.

Cheered by Ackmed's defiance, Matt continues in a voice that borders on being disrespectful. "Ok, your worship, say I accept that your wonderful kingdom is all you say and that your hands are clean. What about the group of whites that were lynched a few weeks ago? What about that girl earlier? Did she give you head out of the kindness of her heart? And to address the white- or if you prefer the black- elephant in the room, what about us? You kept us in an uncomfortable, unheated hanger overnight. A hanger which smelled bad enough to let us know that we weren't the first ones to be held there. If you are so civilized, sir, then please by all means explain away those simple facts."

I manage to stay silent this time, but I recognize the great counter-point that Matt just delivered. I had no idea he was such a great writer. It's like watching an episode of *Law and Order*.

"The groups of whites you refer are members of the First Baptist Church. They attacked us without provocation. Killing them was excusable, but the manner in which they were killed was not. The leader of that group has been punished for his actions. And, may I say, Matthew, you have my deepest condolences on the loss of your brother."

Thaddeus looks pleased with the startled reactions that we all wear as he reveals Matt's true identity. "It was erroneously reported to me that you were members of that same radical group. As we are at war with them, you were treated as prisoners of war rather than honored guests. For that, I must beg forgiveness. I am currently in the process of discovering exactly where the breakdown in communication occurred. Rest assured that when I do, those responsible will be….dealt with. As you attacked my guards when they came to escort you, they were forced to use rubber bullets to subdue you."

For a moment, I think that Thaddeus intends to ignore the issue of the girl. It is difficult for anyone to justify what amounts to rape, but to my shock, Thaddeus continues. "That girl sacrificed her body for the greater good."

We all respond at the same time. "The greater good."

Fortunately, Thaddeus seems to think that it is a question. He answers it with another question. "Indeed. Let me pose a question to you gentlemen. Say that you were in charge of a group of men living in a society that forces them to kill often. Many of these men are violent criminals. What would you do to keep them following you?"

I think immediately of the TV show *OZ*. "You have to be just as brutal as they are."

Thaddeus sounds like a professor as he smiles and sits back in his chair. "Correct, Malcolm. While I physically did enjoy the oral sex, I am morally repulsed by the thought of forcing any woman, regardless of her color, to perform a sex act against her will. However, it is a necessary evil. The men that brought you here must see that I am brutal. They must go tell the other men that follow me what an evil bastard I am. My utter lack of regard for whites, at least in the society we used to live in, is best personified by forcing a white woman to have sex with me. It must appear to them, and you, as if she was forced to stay here. In reality, she was given the option to stay here as my concubine or leave my kingdom. She chooses to stay."

Thaddeus leans in, as if telling us a secret. "Being my concubine is not all that bad. She shares her quarters with me, and I am a gentle man. She is not beaten or abused in any way. I am actually quite fond of Michelle, and I believe that she feels the same. The only caveat to our relationship is that periodically, she must give me a blowjob in public. And every couple of months, she must change the color of her hair."

"Her hair?"

Thaddeus smiles genuinely. "You white people all look alike, so if her hair changes, my men assume that I have multiple concubines."

Albert brings in a plate of steaks. My stomach growls in anticipation. Thaddeus gets served first, then motions for us to eat once the steaks are in front of us. "One day, I hope that such brutal tactics will not be necessary. Now, to address the big black elephant in the room. What are a group of filmmakers and the son of preacher doing in my kingdom?"

EIGHTEEN

"Did you tell him the truth?" Sam looks at me as if this is some sort of test. Women love honesty. I have to impress her.

"I always tell the truth." Sam purses her lips and raises an eyebrow. Perhaps I had been too truthful. No one is ever all anything. I feel like I am failing the test. "Well, most of the time anyway. Always to people that I care about."

We are both silent for a time, and my cheeks begin to flush. Perhaps that had been a going a bit too far. I had just met Sam. "Besides, what could endear me more to a black supremacist than rescuing a black woman? Also, he could have figured out the truth easily enough. I didn't want to get caught lying to a king."

We both laugh, and the test feeling ended. I think that I passed.

"So did he send you on your way?"

"Not right away. He loved the concept of our mission, and vowed to help us in any way he could."

"So you were happily allied with a rapist and murderer?" Sam looks disapproving again. Time for test number two.

"I still questioned his methods and morality. Hell, I didn't even like the guy all that much. Rape is always wrong, and most of the time, so is murder. I respect the hell out of women and-" I stop, and realize that I have been rambling. Sam is grinning a bit, because it is obvious that she has made me uncomfortable. Test number two passed.

"Regardless of his morals, Thaddeus did serve some good steak. They also had these little pieces of potato that had been fried in olive oil and spices. After not eating for the better part of a day, it was wonderful. After breakfast Thaddeus reunited us with a delighted J'Marcus, who led us to our sleeping quarters. Our quarters were the first class section of a broken 747. There were beds there to accommodate rich people on long flights to Tokyo or England or something. It was cramped, and the beds were lumpy. Compared to the cold hanger, however, it felt like I was sleeping on a cloud. I slept for a full day, and it was the best sleep I had ever had." I lean back, proud of my description.

"I don't think that I could sleep that well in the middle of the apocalypse."

"You should have seen the security. It was Death Star like. Guards were everywhere- and there was no zombie that reminded me of Obi-Wan Kenobi or Han Solo, so I felt safe." I waited. They say that women test men, but men test women as well, and this was my test.

Sam laughs and brushes her hair back. "So there were no boring conversations or talk of T16's?"

Test passed. "Nope. Unlike Imperial Stormtroopers these guards looked precise and competent."

"I always wondered how Stormtroopers could be trained so well, and suck so badly. An old man and a farmer beat them all." Sam giggles, and looks cute doing it too. Being cute and knowledgeable about <u>Star Wars</u> gets Sam extra credit on my test.

"What happened with Ackmed? Was it an epic confrontation?" Sam had just gotten herself bonus points for using epic in a sentence.

"Surprisingly no. He didn't really want to lead, for all his posturing in the hanger. Even though he pretended to lead, he often deferred to one of us, and tended to ask our opinions a lot. It seemed like we were all in control, which was fine by me. I am perfectly fine with compromise."

I smile confidently. I am so good with women. They love men that can compromise. Secure in the knowledge that I had hooked Sam into my story by describing my wonderful personality, I continue. "Everything was going great. Thaddeus washed our clothes for us and gave us back the meager amount of supplies that we had grabbed from the truck. We were living well in the airport- they still had really great fast food. But, as with everything, it needed to end. On the evening of our second night, over a dinner of McDonald's chicken nuggets and French fries, Thaddeus asked us what our plans were...."

■■

None of us respond right away. The last two days had been fantastic. I dip my chicken nugget into some honey and swirl it around for a while like a salsa shark. "Well, I guess we are going to go after the First Lady. Probably tomorrow morning after breakfast."

Thaddeus grunts. "Good. I am enjoying your company, but as I said before, you people are only allowed to live with us for limited amounts of time."

He continues to justify kicking us out, but I am not listening. I am cataloging the pitiful pile of supplies that had been returned to us with our clean laundry. There are three pistols, two rifles, my axe, and Ackmed's Katana. We have a pathetic amount of ammo- about twenty rounds for each pistol, and ten for each rifle. Kevin got his camera back, and had spent the entire day walking around Thaddeus's compound recording and interviewing. I didn't help. The website and the movie seemes far away and unimportant now.

At least my zombie shirt is clean.

After dinner, the four of us sit in the 747, talking softly. Ackmed wants to go home, Matt wants to rescue Brian, and Kevin wants to go after Crystal. It is an impasse. Since this is now a collaborative effort, my opinion is the deciding factor. I like being somewhat in charge of the plot.

"I think that we should go after Crystal." I wait for the inevitable eruption of anger from Ackmed, but he just nods, realizing that he has been outvoted.

"What about weapons?" Ackmed may agree in principal with following us, but he is going to do his best to poke holes in our plans. He sits back, looking sure of himself.

Before I can answer, J'Marcus walks into our temporary home. He has on headphones and is singing a song by *Mindless Self Indulgence*. Taking off his headphones, he smiles at the group warmly. "I brought cookies."

J'Marcus holds up a blue package and tosses it to Ackmed. All of us ignore the action. I would love a cookie, but the weapons are a much more pressing concern. J'Marcus opens the package and takes a cookie. Making his way to a spare bed, he mumbles, "Don't everybody thank me at once."

J'Marcus had helped Kevin with his filming that morning, so he is the first to speak. "Sorry, J'Marcus. We were just trying to figure out how we can rescue Crystal with so little ammo."

"That's what I came to see you about. I know a way that we can get that ammo." J'Marcus leans back and puts his hands behind his head. He makes the idea of getting the ammo sound like a walk to the grocery store.

"We?" Ackmed, despite his development, regression, and development again is still suspicious of strangers.

"Well, if you will have me. I don't exactly fit in here." J'Marcus proceeds to tell us that most of the tough men with Thaddeus are criminals. The rest were once honest, hardworking people, but Thaddeus had twisted them into hard men willing to do anything in order to regain the Midwest. J'Marcus is from Philadelphia. All he wants to do is get out of Chicago and go back home.

Ackmed grants permission for J'Marcus to accompany us, which is good because Kevin looks so stoked about him joining us that Ackmed would have been in for a fight had he chosen otherwise. Kevin gives J'Marcus a hug. I shake his hand, and Matt nods. Ackmed is more practical, though. "Where can we get those weapons at?"

"The armory on 55th street. It's in Hyde Park, right by the Brackley's house. There should be tons of National Guard weapons there."

"How do we get from here to there?" I am practical too. That is why I am a good leader.

J'Marcus looks at me like I am an idiot. Scoffing a bit, he shrugs his shoulders. "We walk."

■■

I feel good. I am warm, dressed in clean clothes, and my stomach is full of pancakes and sausage. The weather has unexpectedly turned bright and sunny, with the temperature hovering about 55 degrees. All in all, it is not a bad day for Chicago in November. I feel as far away from that terrible night in the hanger as I can.

Except that I am standing in front of the same gray gate that I entered two days ago. It is the night after we came up with our insane plan to raid the armory. What seemed great over cookies now seems impossible. But, we have no choice. If we don't leave soon, Thaddeus will kick us out.

Last night, after J'Marcus joined us, we decided on a definitive plan. Matt, who is concerned about his friend, will part ways with us. I had created a story for Matt involving his abduction by Thaddeus's men; it is so real a story that even I believe it.

Meanwhile, while Matt returns to the Church, we will proceed to Hyde Park. Once Crystal is rescued, we can come back to the safe house where Michael had found us. In exactly one week, we will meet up with Matt, Brian, and Brian's wife.

J'Marcus will come with us. After we agree to bring him, he lets us know that in Philadelphia, he is a volunteer EMT. It seems that I have formed quite a party. Ackmed is our melee specialist, Matt is our ranged attacker, and J'Marcus is our healer. Kevin makes movie magic, so that makes him our magician.

Which brings me back to the gate. Ten feet of dark gray concrete, it has a small strip of yellow running along the top of it. Two days ago, this gate represented a reprieve from the monsters outside. It represented a chance to rest. Now, I am going back out into the city.

Inside the compound is safety and security. Both of those things are taken away as the door slowly opens with a screech.

"See you in a week." Ackmed shakes hands with Matt. He turns to me. With a grin, he asks, "You ready?"

I look at my party. Kevin hugs Matt. J'Marcus stands to the side with Michael and Malcolm, who have come to escort us to the edge of Thaddeus's territory. Ackmed looks ahead through the gate. His jaw is set and he looks confident. I feel as if I should make some sort of speech. Nothing comes to mind, so I check my rifle and begin to walk through the gate. "Nope."

The safety is off, and we are headed east.

The next half day is somewhat anti climactic. Utilizing the ladder system to travel, we cover about eight blocks with relative ease. At about noon we part ways with Michael and Malcolm, promising to stop by the compound and say goodbye on our way out of the city. As they disappear over a building, I stand in the middle of the deserted four lane road that 55th Street has become.

"Well, we are on our own now." Kevin takes in the parked cars and dark shops lining the street. Nothing moves, and not even birds chirp. This is the heart of the concrete jungle- no trees are visible for several blocks. "It's quiet."

"Too quiet." J'Marcus begins to walk, and we follow.

"There is nothing funny about bad prose." I speak a bit too harshly, so I add, "After all you in particular should want to avoid clichés. The black dude always dies in these stories."

J'Marcus smiles, but looks uncomfortable. I want to apologize, but I don't. Guilt begins to creep into my stomach and neck, making me want to itch. I should not have yelled at J'Macus, even though predictable writing is a crime against literature.

The first zombie appears at about 4:30, just as the sun is beginning to set. The beautiful temperatures have dropped to the low 40's. I want to get inside before it gets dark. Kevin notices the approaching figure first. "Zombie."

Ackmed begins to draw his sword and walk forward. Baring his path, I look at him seriously. "Remember what happened last time."

"What happened last time?" Kevin begins to tell J'Marcus about the first zombie that we encountered upon our arrival in Chicago.

Ackmed interrupts before the story is finished. "I remember Malcolm. Strictly beheadings from now on, I think."

The zombie, a Mexican man wearing a soccer shirt, limps onwards. His howl is cut short by Ackmed's katana slicing through his vocal chords. Soccer Fan's head rolls down the street a few feet, stopping behind the tire of a Chevy Venture minivan, causing its alarm to begin screeching.

The noise sounds like an early warning siren, the kind that they use to announce tornados.

"Shit, they must have heard that." Kevin lowers his camera. I hadn't even seen him take it out, but there it is, recording everything for posterity.

I search frantically for a building suitable to sleep in overnight. The closest is a Burger King on the corner of Western and 55th. The lights are off, but all the windows are intact. "Let's get it our way."

We run to the restaurant, locking the door behind us. Nothing moves inside, although the building smells like rotting flesh. The tables contain used wrappers that tell the story of half eaten meals interrupted. Dead flies litter the tables and floor in droves. They must have been attracted by the prospect of an easy meal when it was warm out, only to die of the cold during the fall.

The smell of the building is bad, but the kitchen is worse. Grease has been left in the fryer, and flies cover every inch of the floor. Ackmed takes charge of our group. "J'Marcus, see if you can find a broom and sweep these flies up. "

Mumbling something about being the slave of the group, J'Marcus disappears into the janitor's closet. "Kevin, see if there is any food here while Malcolm and I block the doors."

Pushing garbage cans in front of the doors and hoping that they will be heavy enough to stop any zombies, I spot the first of the approaching horde. There are literally hundreds of them coming at us. We quickly reenter the kitchen, out of view of the windows. J'Marcus is furiously sweeping fly bodies into a neat pile near the corner of the room. It is about two inches high and a foot long. Ackmed tell J'Marcus to relax and begins to sweep up the room. Kevin reports that there is no food. We settle down behind the counter and wait.

■ ■

My feet feel like they are going to fall off. I remove my shoes and rub the blisters that are forming. It feels good to be doing anything other than walking. My legs and knees feel like they are made of linguini. I close my eyes and reflect on the fact that walking the entire day sucks.

My feet smell like a combination of sweat and general foot odor. Initially, I am horrified by the smell. Not that the restaurant smells good, but I am not thrilled at adding to the general stench. I am about to reluctantly pull my shoes back on when I notice that everyone else is in the same position I am.

Kevin is also rubbing his feet. "Man, walking sucks."

"We could try driving again. If the closest horde just passed us, we might be able to drive the rest of the way." Ackmed always liked racing games.

Before I can even talk about the risks, Kevin agrees. "This Lord of the Rings shit sucks. There's too much walking."

"Speaking of Lord of the Rings, I think that I'm the ranger of this group. After all, I've been living out here in the wilderness the longest." J'Marcus makes an interesting point, and I am glad to see him joining in our banter.

"If anyone is Aragon, I am Aragon." Ackmed puffs his chest. "Are you frightened? Not nearly frightened enough."

I agree. I may be the most interesting character, but Ackmed is definitely the hero. Still, I can't let him get a big head. "I would say you're more like Gimley."

"Seriously, though. Do we need to walk anymore? Even if we don't run into trouble, it is going to be a while before we get there."

I am hopelessly out of shape. I really need to start working out.

J'Marcus begins to speak, but is interrupted by Ackmed. "We could try a car, but where would we get one with keys? None of us can hotwire a car." We all lapse into our own version of the thinking man.

"Guys." J'Marcus begins, but I am not really listening. He is for sure not the writer of the group; at best, he is a minor character that is easily disposable. His plans and opinions don't count yet.

"I suppose we could break into a house and try to find a set of spare keys to a car." I sound so doubtful that even I don't believe that it is a good idea. Like I said, I hate clearing houses.

"Guys, I think I have an idea." J'Marcus's voice approaches a scream of frustration.

We all turn to look at him, and he points above our heads. Carefully peaking above the counter, I see a car repair shop across the street. "Hey, there is a repair shop across the street."

"I bet one of those cars works, and they have the keys to them locked up inside. Right across the street." Kevin sounds proud, and J'Marcus shakes his head in exasperation.

"That's what I've been trying to say." J'Marcus screams so loud that we shush him.

"That's a great idea, J'Marcus." I smile so that he knows we had been kidding with him.

"Thanks. Now, here's the plan. I will sneak out there and pick the lock on the gate once this horde passes us. Then, I can grab some keys and head over with the car." Maybe J'Marcus is a writer after all.

"Pick the lock? I thought you were a healer man. Pick a class, dude." Ackmed shakes his head.

"I had a mis-spent youth." J'Marcus shrugs like it is no big deal.

I am suddenly very curious about the dark man sitting in front of me. "J'Marcus, what's your story?"

J'Marcus shakes his head and looks at the floor. "It's not that interesting."

"It's important we get to know you. We are, after all, fighting on the same side. Tell us about yourself."

••

J'Marcus' story is difficult to follow, mainly because we have to ask him questions to get him to talk. It seems that talking about his past makes him shy.

Rather than tell you exactly what he said, I will use my writing skills to edit what J'Marcus said into an understandable synopsis. (If any editors are reading this, I should probably tell you that I am available and open to employment opportunities.)

From the time he was about 15, J'Marcus stole things. Not so much for the thrill, although that was certainly part of it, but to survive. With two parents that were never home, J'Marcus started out stealing food, and gradually moved on to clothes. Once the basics of survival were covered, he started stealing things he wanted, like electronics and video games. It was this electronic equipment that captured the eye of a local thief, Norman. Norman took J'Marcus under his wing and taught him to really steal. Norman ran a crew of serious thieves- they did not steal TV's and VCR's from homes. They stole entire pallets of merchandise. They broke into banks and unlocked safes. They were smart, and not flashy or loose with their money. In fact, Norman encouraged the thieves to improve themselves. J'Marcus invested some of the money he made and earned a bachelor's degree in graphic design. He drew his final designs on a supercomputer that the group stole. Norman also encouraged savings, and the entire group hid a percentage of their money in a secret location.

In short, they were very good at what they did, and that is what got them caught. Their heists were so impressive that the city of Philadelphia formed a task force to catch them. It was only a matter of time, and one day the task force closed in on the group. The police arrested everyone as they planned a job in their warehouse base. The only reason that J'Marcus escaped was because he was not at the meeting; he was chasing a girl named Emily at the time.

With his entire crew in jail, J'Marcus took the kitty that they had saved out of hiding. Inside was roughly a million dollars. Newly rich, J'Marcus did what anyone that had that kind of money would do: he retired to a beach in Mexico at the ripe old age of 26.

It didn't work out with Emily.

That would have been the end of it, except that J'Marcus got bored. He missed the thrill of the heist. As he put it, "The butterflies in your stomach stop flying around and you do something totally incredible, like unlock a bank safe or break into a warehouse." J'Marcus wanted the thrill, but didn't want to go to prison. When J'Marcus visited Norman in prison, he told him to, "go straight because jail sucks." As he was leaving the prison, J'Marcus saw an ambulance and had an idea.

Not wanting to give up his lifestyle of his art, J'Marcus began taking classes to become a paramedic while he worked full time designing pictures and websites. The training was quick, barely two years, and on the ambulance J'Marcus found the thrill of doing something incredible again. The best part of working as a paramedic was that it was legal. There was no chance of going to prison.

J'Marcus had been in Chicago securing a contract to design a pornography website. He was even going to draw some pictures of absurdly unrealistic and disproportional women doing nasty things. Before his flight could leave, the zombies attacked.

When we asked him why he threw his lot in with us, J'Marcus replied, "Well I am a nerd. One of the first things that I stole was VCR and a copy of <u>Star Wars THX</u>. I think that I fit in better with you."

Thus J'Marcus joined our group officially. In the time it took him to tell his past, J'Marcus transformed himself from a minor player to a main character in our story. He possessed his own set of skills. He was now a deeper character, and no longer expendable.

When J'Marcus finishes the story, it is completely dark. Sinking back onto the uncomfortable floor, I attempt to ignore the way the tile floor digs into my back. Still, the Burger King is warm, so it is a vast improvement over the warehouse. The others are snoring softly. Combined with the sound of the zombies outside moaning, it makes for an incredible chorus. If my book ever gets turned into a movie, I want there to be a better soundtrack.

My thoughts wander, and I dream of Hester. She is holding a gun, firing into a crowd of zombies that is about to overwhelm her. I am helping Kevin shoot a scene for our movie. Turning to me, Hester screams for help, but I am too far away to save her. The zombies surround her, and the last words she shouts are accusatory. "You picked Crystal over me."

I wake with a start. The zombies still howl, and my friends still snore. I shift a little and try to think of the positive things that will happen tomorrow. Tomorrow we will be in the safety of a car. With any luck, we will also reequip ourselves with government property. Tomorrow will be the first day of the rest of our lives.

Outside, the zombies continue to howl. I close my eyes, but do not sleep well.

NINETEEN

By the time the morning sun vanquishes the terrible night, the zombies have disappeared. The temperature now hovers around 30 degrees. That is not all that cold, but when combined with the pounding rain, it makes my nipples feel like they are going to pop out of my shirt. I feel the same way about our plan to get the car. On the surface, it seems really simple; J'Marcus simply needed to cross the street and get a car. In reality, though, it is not that simple at all.

The sky itself is filled with contradictions. Although the East shows no clouds, the skies directly above us are black and threatening.   Rain drips down, not fast, but steady enough to make me shiver as I open the door and let J'Marcus outside.   I had wanted to wait outside until J'Marcus made it across the street, but the rain is so miserable that after he takes two steps, I flee back into the warm Burger King.

Ackmed, Kevin, and I watch J'Marcus walk across the street, not varying his gate even due to the rain. He bends over the massive padlock that holds the chain link fence surrounding the auto shop. I have no idea what he does, but within seconds J'Marcus pulls the lock open and slides the gate to the side. He disappears into the yard, hidden from view by various vans and trucks scattered throughout the yard.

We sit in a booth covered with dead flies, staring out the window into the gloomy morning. The drizzle turns to a steady rain, which clinks on the roof like a thousand different BB's hitting us every second. As the wind picks up, the windows rattle loudly as they attempt to brave the gale.

Still we wait. Every tick of the clock seems to take a full minute. With every second that passes by, all I can imagine are the things that can go wrong with this plan. There could be zombies in the shop, left over from the horde that had passed us during the night. How they could have picked the lock and ventured inside is beyond me, but it is possible. The horde could be following some kind of odd migration pattern, like a flock of birds. They could return at any time. J'Marcus could slip in the rain and fall. Crossing the street is dangerous during the best of times. Every day, hundreds of people in the world attempt to cross a street only to have their day rudely interrupted by a bus.

Still we wait, peering into the street and searching for any sign of life. A short yellow bus, the kind that "special" kids ride in, slowly lurches out of the yard and turns toward us. J'Marcus, clearly enjoying himself, opens the side door and waves to us. The bus's diesel engine hums along, giving us instant background music.

We climb in the bus. Ackmed regards J'Marcus with a raised eyebrow. "The short bus?"

"It seems appropriate." J'Marcus closes the door and the bus jerks into first gear. I fall backward, into a seat. Sitting up, I notice everyone else also laying in seats. J'Marcus begins to sing in a surprisingly listenable voice. "The wheels on the bus go round and round, round and round."

Kevin moves a seat up, so he is directly behind J'Marcus. "You're having fun with this, aren't you?"

We all sit down in the front seats. It is probably the first time that I have ever sat in the front of the bus. When I was a kid, it was much easier to sit in the back and cause trouble. By causing trouble, I mean do such hair raising things as playing *Magic the Gathering* and getting the shit beat out of me by people twice my size. And I thought that my giant foam sword from D and D would make me intimidating.

Now, I hold an axe, and am quite intimidating. Or at least I think so.

The bus rolls along at a quick pace. We have already covered five or six blocks in the short time that we have been moving. The city is deserted, and being on the road reminds me of the feeling you get when driving around late at night on a big holiday like Christmas. Nothing moves, and the world seems just empty. There are no zombies at all. The engine continues to provide a rhythm for us and is joined by the rain drumming on the roof.

A half hour later, we arrive at the armory. I have never really paid attention to the wonder of modern technology. I just sort of took it for granted. The automobile, even a crappy little school bus, is a wonderful invention. If we had walked to the armory, it would have taken us at least a day or two. We would have arrived wet and tired, and possibly had to fight off zombies on the way. The bus, however, got us to the armory in as much time as it takes to solve a crime on TV's Castle. To top it off, I find that I am not really all that tired as we pull up to the decrepit gray building with a sign that reads US Army National Guard. A statue carved into the building depicts a World War I soldier holding a rifle with a bayonet attached to it. He looks ready to challenge anyone who doesn't belong there, even though his eyes are lifeless gray. The somewhat normal looking double door under the soldier is less imposing, and within no time, J'Marcus picks the lock and we walk in.

The inside of the building is standard Government issue. The walls are white, although here and there, the color has faded over time into a light yellow. Posters exulting the virtues of the National Guard's college education repayment program line the walls. The floor is white tile, spotless and clean.

The building looks as if it hasn't been touched. If the National Guard had called on its soldiers, none of them had made it here. Helpful signs point the way to the armory, which turns out to be a room with a window that has a cage around it. We carefully break into the door next to the window. What we find inside may be the closest thing to sexy that I have ever seen.

The room is full of guns. Lots of guns. M16's, M16's with grenade launchers, Squad Automatic Weapons (SAW's), and even two M60 machine guns rest in nooks cut into the wall. There are so many weapons that the wall itself appears to be made out of dark black metal.

Ackmed opens a case to reveal explosives. We search all the similar cases that litter the room. There are smoke grenades, frag grenades, claymore mines, and rocket launchers. It is like Christmas at Ted Nugent's house.

"We are going to be unstoppable." Ackmed picks up an M16 and strokes it contentedly, the way normal people stroke a lover.

"Do you guys know how to use any of these things?" J'Marcus pries open a container marked MRE's.

I pick up a combat shotgun and cock it dramatically. "I'm a Colonel in Call of Duty. I have virtually fired every one of these."

Ackmed has switched and is now cradling a 26 pound SAW like it is a baby. "Plus, we are not exactly morons in the gun department. Except for Malcolm. He can't shoot shit."

"That's why I have the shotgun. I won't have to aim, just point it in the general direction and pull the trigger."

J'Marcus holds up a brown pouch, and then tosses it to me. "Well then Colonel, with your extensive military experience you should know what one of these are."

I don't know what it is, but J'Marcus explains that it is an MRE, which is basically 3500 self heating calories in a brown bag. I am delighted, as I have had nothing to eat since leaving the airport yesterday morning. The beef and carrots are fantastic, rivaling any fancy steak restaurant. The M and M's taste better than anything the chefs on Cupcake Wars can dream of.

Kevin leans back and belches. "Happy Thanksgiving."

Ackmed pats his belly. "It's not Thanksgiving."

"No, but it is November, and we just stuffed ourselves on food, which I am thankful for. So happy Thanksgiving." It sounds stupid, but as Kevin opens another MRE and fishes out a Reese's Peanut Butter Cup, the thought of overeating appeals to me

"Maybe we shouldn't call it Thanksgiving. If we call it something else, we can eat way too much in a couple of weeks too. I open up my own brown bag and end up with a bag of Skittles.

"How about Happy Ammo Day?" It is hard to understand J'Marcus because he has an entire Snickers bar in his mouth.

"No." Ackmed lifts up one a big green tube that is undoubtedly a bazooka. "Happy Rocket Launcher Day."

Everyone replies at once. "Happy Rocket Launcher Day."

■■■

It is still mid morning, so we decide to explore the building a bit. Happy Rocket Launcher Day becomes Happy Body Armor Day when we find new army uniforms. Afterwards, we shower and shave (all except for Kevin, who stoically continues to wear his filmmaker beard.) I feel pretty military. J'Marcus pins an eagle insignia on my new hat, making me officially a Colonel.

I wonder if my promotion means that I am back in charge of the group.

Happy Body Armor day becomes Happy Hummer Day when we find a fully functional Hummer in the parking lot. A terrifyingly huge .50 caliber machine gun sticks out the back of the Hummer.

Happy Machine Gun Day.

Although it is tempting to abandon the ridiculous yellow bus, I know that we will need the space. Making off color and offensive jokes the whole time, we load the small bus with as many weapons as we can fit inside and set off. Ackmed and I ride in the Hummer, while Kevin and J'Marcus ride in the bus. I realize that we are in a convoy, and immediately begin singing until Ackmed tells me to shut up.

Hyde Park is an odd area of Chicago. Parts of it, like the area we are currently in have homes with broken windows and chipping paint. Old four story brick apartments rise on the street corners, framing the houses in the middle like bookends. Black bars made of steel protect the windows in stores named things like Mamma D's Chicken and Rib Tips or Latisha's Salon and Beauty shop. Old liquor bottles and paper bags from fast food restaurants lay in the street.

This goes on as we head east on 55th Street. Eventually, the road begins to curve through the actual park portion of Hyde Park. Trees grow tall on either side of the road. The green of overgrown grass peeks out from under layers of brown leaves that have fallen to the ground.

Benches litter the park, and on our right a slate gray building with tennis courts and basketball hoops sits dormant.

A few solitary zombies roam the area, shuffling back and forth through ankle high grass. None of them turn to face us, so we do our best to ignore them as we continue through the park.

The neighborhood changes again. Tall modern buildings with large windows make up the University of Chicago Hospital and school campus. Surrounding the hospital, older gothic buildings with huge buttresses of brownstone proclaim their importance on signs that read things like Resident Hall and Law School. Zombies wander about these buildings wearing hospital scrubs and ID cards around their necks.

As we turn down a side street, older brick homes appear. Many of them serve as faculty residences. These buildings are different than the ones we passed earlier. There are no bars on the windows here, and the porches are neat. (If you overlook the blood and body parts splattered everywhere.) No litter blows around on the ground, and while the lawns are a bit overgrown, they look to have been well maintained before the zombies arrives.

Then, we see them. About 20 zombies surround a house near the end of the block. These zombies are not wandering around aimlessly; they moan and groan, but appear to have a purpose. They claw at the windows of the house, desperate to get inside.

"Are we there yet?" Ackmed, sitting in the gunner seat, impatiently pulls a lever on the gun. It clicks ominously as he cocks it, as if telling the world that it is ready to destroy something.

"We are here." I indicate the house that the zombies have surrounded.

I am just opening the door when Ackmed begins shooting. The machine gun makes a huge noise, like a small thunderstorm. I begin to aim my shotgun, but quickly lower it. It isn't needed; the zombies are literally being ripped apart by the impact. Gray flesh flies two feet in the air as the bullets strike home. Ackmed smiles and laughs as zombies' limbs are torn from their bodies. The machine gun rocks him back and forth slowly due to the recoil, making it look like he is writhing in ecstasy.

Within seconds, all of the zombies are on the ground, although some still struggle to move and bite. The rest lie still. Kevin runs up next to me, holding his rifle. "Holy shit."

The door to the house opens and a man walks out. He wears running pants and a University of Chicago tee-shirt. He is well built, large and strong looking with closely cropped hair. "Way to go Colonel. Get some."

Picking through the bodies, the man pumps his fist into the air. "Not that I am complaining or anything, but what are you doing here?"

"Happy Machine Gun Day." Kevin points at the Hummer. "We are just here to wish you a Happy Machine Gun Day."

The man frowns in confusion and tilts his head to the side, like a dog that doesn't quite understand what is going on. Taking advantage of his distraction, one of the zombies at his feet stirs. He is a newly legless corpse with long dark hair and a black ACDC shirt. He reaches up with a rotten hand and bites through the man's leg even as J'Marcus splits his head open like a melon with his M16.

None of us know what to say. The man is surely going to die; he has just been bitten by a zombie. We are saved from any awkward conversation by the appearance of another zombie, who wanders around in the fenced yard next door. He is balding and wears a tattered suit.

Ackmed aims the machine gun, but the man who was bitten stops him. "Wait, he's the Ambassador from South Africa. We haven't done anything about him yet, because he has diplomatic immunity."

"It's just been revoked." The diplomat seems to explode as Ackmed holds the trigger down for a full ten seconds.

"What the hell is wrong with you? You just caused an international incident. Colonel, I demand that you punish this man." The doomed man is furious. He seems to have odd priorities. If I were bitten by a zombie, I would be more concerned about the fact that I was going to die soon, and probably never going to get laid again.

"The only good zombie is a dead zombie." Ackmed is enjoying this John Wayne routine a bit too much.

The man ignores Ackmed. Instead he points over his shoulder at the house. "Colonel, we should probably get inside before more show up."

We carefully cross the steaming pit of zombies, pausing only to fire into the ones that still move, and enter the house.

A handsome black woman of about forty greets me. She is wearing a sweatshirt with the White House on it and tights. I recognize her as Crystal Brackley, the First Lady. She looks me up and down. Despite the differences in our age, I am a bit taken aback and uncomfortable. For lack of a better term, this chick is a MILF. And she is checking me out. Like the Rooster Teeth shirt says, "I don't like it when girls pay attention to me." I begin to flush.

As she studies me, a half smile appears on her face. It is a bratty smile that I recognize well from the mean girls I encountered in high school. When she speaks, it is in a voice that reminds me of a spoiled girl. "Aren't you a little young to be a Colonel?"

TWENTY

I am confused. "Huh?"

Wordlessly, Crystal points to the eagle on my uniform.

"Oh, the uniform. I'm Malcolm Tushton. I'm here to rescue you."

Her voice rises in concern. "You're who?"

"I'm from the internet. Grant sent me."

"So, if you're not military, who are you and where did you get that uniform? And on whose authority did you just murder a diplomat?" The man who was bitten outside pauses, then turns to Crystal. "They shot the South African Diplomat."

Ackmed takes a step forward. "What business of it is yours?"

"Agent Anderson, US Secret Service." Anderson flips out his wallet which has a little plastic ID holder. His voice has the arrogant quality that all law enforcement types seem to learn at the academy.

J'Marcus seems to bristle at the arrogance. Acting on some sort of forgotten criminal instinct, he raises his rifle. "You ain't gonna be shit except for a dead motherfucker with a hole in his head from this."

"Are you threatening me?"

"Ain't no need to threaten you. You a dead man walking."

Either Ackmed is writing the bad prose again, or cops really bring out the ghetto side of J'Marcus.

Kevin points at the man and says tenderly, "He is right. You were bitten."

I had forgotten about the bite, but J'Marcus hadn't. Patting his rifle, he continues in an evil voice. "Don't you worry though Mr. Secret Service Agent, I won't let you hurt anyone. When you turn, I will take care of you."

"When I turn?" Anderson looks at Crystal and laughs. "When I turn."

Crystal rolls her eyes.

Kevin places his hand on Anderson's shoulder reassuringly. "Ok, you are experiencing the stage of grief known as…." Kevin pauses as if he is thinking. "Um, hilarity. Yeah, the hilarity stage of grief. That's the stage where the thought of death makes you, uh, crack up.

The whole room stops. Anderson stops laughing, J'Marcus stops posturing and Crystal stops rolling her eyes. Everyone looks at Kevin and in unison replies, "What?"

"The stages of grief. Mr. Anderson- or maybe I should say Agent Anderson- is grieving for his loss, in this case himself. There are stages to that grief. What are you all looking at? It's a thing." Kevin suddenly looks uncomfortable with the whole room staring at him. Maybe I should loan him my Rooster Teeth shirt.

"I think you mean acceptance." J'Marcus regards Anderson suspiciously. "But since Agent Anderson here appears to think his death is funny, I would say that he is in denial."

"I'm not in denial because there is nothing to deny." Anderson seems to puff up more, as if his explanation should awe us.

Maybe I, as an English major, can explain a bit better. "Saying something that is plainly there and then denying that you are in denial is kind of the definition of denial."

"I swear I am going to shoot the next person that says denial." Crystal raises her pistol.

Anderson leans close to me, and puts his face directly in mine, like we are on a playground somewhere. "Who are you to tell me what is real, you fake Colonel?"

"Back off man, I'm a writer."

"Everybody just calm down." Kevin raises his hands above his head and brings them down, as if that will calm us down. "We are here to help. We got the guns from the Army. Just trust me. Now, if I may ask, what is so funny about your imminent departure from this earth?"

"For the sake of time, I'll accept your explanation for now. I expect a more detailed one later. As far as my condition goes, I am not in-" he glances warily at Crystal- "denial. The zombies don't turn me. I don't turn into a zombie."

"What do you turn into then? Not one of those gay vampires from <u>Twilight</u>?" I want to calm the room down a bit too, so I hope my joke works.

"Nope. I don't turn into anything."

I hear J'Marcus mumble something about him turning into an asshole, so I quickly ask, "Why don't you turn? How many times have you been bitten?"

As an answer, Anderson removes his shirt. He is in great shape, with bulging veins and rippling muscles. Scars, dark and jagged, run up and down his forearms. Most of the scars are formless and could have come from anything, but on his right side just under his neck, they form a small outline of a human mouth.

"The bites heal, but they all scar. Must be something to do with the virus." Noticing our stares, Anderson points to the scar on his neck. "This one here came close. I almost bled to death. If she wasn't a kid, she would have gotten my jugular vein."

"It must be an immunity type of thing." J'Marcus speaks calmly now, like a medical professional. "It's possible that he has some sort of genetic mutation or natural immunity. Every disease has some people that don't get sick from it. Agent Anderson must be one of the lucky few that are immune."

"Yeah, but I get the flu all the time, so it evens out." Anderson grins at his joke, which in truth isn't that funny.

"So you're some kind of XMan with a genetic mutation? That's cool as hell." Kevin turns to J'Marcus. "We are traveling with a mutant that has super powers. This is an awesome party. Good roll."

"Yep, I'm a superhero." Anderson sounds bored. "What do you mean by good party?"

"It's a <u>D and D</u> reference, you wouldn't get it." J'Marcus is still mad about the cop's arrogance.

"You're right, I wouldn't. But, back to the matter at hand. I've shown you mine. Why don't you show me yours, and tell me how you got those weapons?"

• •

"So that's how we got these weapons, and how I am a Colonel." I tap the eagle on my hat.

We are sitting around a wooden table in the Brackley's dining room. The table has a white lace cloth with flowers sewn into it draped over the table. It reminds me of something that my grandma would have. In the corner, a small fireplace provides light and heat. The house smells like cinnamon. You can tell that a woman lives here.

"So what's the plan?" The speaker is a short haired non descript man named Clause. He is another Secret Service agent, although he seems a bit nicer and more respectful. When I told them how I got the weapons from the Army, he even looked a bit impressed, while Anderson only scowled.

I don't quite know how to say that I have no plan. I am afraid that they will freak out. With no ideas forming, I sit in silence and curse my writer's block. Luckily, Ackmed takes over writing this scene for me. "Well, we are really open to suggestion about that."

Anderson sounds appalled. "You came in here and you didn't have a plan for getting out?"

"He's the brains." Ackmed points at me. Just when I thought we were a team.

Kevin, who cares more about what people think than Ackmed and I, interjects. "There wasn't really time to plan anything. We've had a rough couple of weeks just getting here."

Crystal glances pointedly at Anderson and J'Marcus, her gaze warning them not to get into another dick measuring contest. "It hasn't been easy on anyone, but that's not the point. We need to figure this out so we can get out of here. Does anyone have any suggestions?"

"We could take a boat. We are right by the lake. Now that there are more of us here to fight the zombies and protect the First ady, we might just be able to make it over to the Lake Shore Drive and up to North Pier where the boats are kept." Clause's idea sounds great. A couple of blocks east of us, Lake Shore Drive runs parallel with Lake Michigan. A few miles north of that, near downtown, boats were docked. We could simply take one and drive to Wisconsin.

"We have been over this. None of us know how to drive a boat." Anderson sounds tired.

"Richard said that he could figure it out." When we look confused, Clause turns to us. "Richard is the only other member of our group to survive. He is Crystal's personal pilot. He had guard duty last night, and is asleep, but I am sure he would be interested in this boat idea. He can pilot anything in the air, I am guessing he can drive a boat too."

Anderson stands up. "We can wake him up and ask him again, but I don't want to risk the First Lady's life on a pilot being able to bullshit his way around a boat."

The idea sounds great to me. How hard could it be to drive a boat? A few hours on a pleasure cruise, and then we would be home free. Then Kevin ruins it. "Wait. We can't take a boat."

"If you tell me that you get seasick I am going to punch you." Ackmed should be joking, but the intensity in which he speaks leads me to believe that he is serious. I also am angry. I want to take the easy way out.

Kevin looks at us accusingly. "We can't take a boat out because we have to go back west. Remember our friend Matt?"

Shit. Matt. In all the excitement of actually getting to Crystal, I had forgotten about him. It had been two days since we had parted company, so Matt would be making his escape attempt tonight or the next day.

We explain to the group why we need to go back. Clause nods, and mumbles something about never leaving a friend in need. Crystal doesn't respond, but only looks weary as she stares at the floor.

Only Anderson fights us. He stands up, his voice rising. "Wait a minute. You want me to put the First Lady's life in danger to rescue some sixteen year old kid?"

"No. There is also another man who we haven't met, and his wife." Kevin seems to think this helps, for he smiles uncertainly.

"Oh well, if you haven't met him, then let's go. After all, why wouldn't we want to risk our lives for someone we have never met?"

"We never met you, yet we risked our lives to come here." Ackmed stands too and tenses.

"That's different. You know who Crystal is. No one has ever heard of this Mark person." Anderson looks to Crystal for guidance. She doesn't say anything, continuing to stare at the floor.

Kevin finally shows some frustration. When he speaks, the temperature of the room almost lowers. "His name is Matt. And he is one of the reasons that we were able to get to you in the first place."

Anderson begins to respond, but Crystal interrupts. Looking us in the face, she sighs. "Let's go get your friend. We owe it to him. I am obviously able to defend myself, and I have lasted this long. What are a few more days?"

"M'am, I cannot allow you to-"

"You don't allow me to do anything Agent Anderson. Remember that. I am your superior. Your desire to keep me safe is admirable, and you have done a great job thus far. Remember, though, that I make the decisions. I say let's go as soon as we are packed." When Crystal speaks, I swear the temperature in the room really does go down. Hell hath no fury.

Anderson begins to harp on us for not having an escape plan, but Ackmed holds up his hand. Smiling a half smile that drives women crazy, Ackmed quotes Star Wars. "Wait a minute. I got an idea."

The fire glints off his intelligent eyes, and he tells us his plan.

■■■

Richard wakes up a few hours later. He proves to be a muscular man in his 40's with wavy brown hair and ruggedly handsome features. While he packs his things, we tell him our plan. He listens intently, adding additional witty comments here and there. When we finish explaining, he shrugs. Staring at us with knowing blue eyes, he remarks in a nonchalant way, "I can do it."

His arrogance is different from Anderson's. While Anderson makes you feel like he is entitled to respect, Richard makes you feel safe in the hands of a master. I begin to like him immediately.

It doesn't take long for everyone to get packed. Despite my fears, Crystal chooses to leave all the china and fine jewelry behind, taking only a backpack full of clothes and a shotgun. When I comment on this to Clause, he nods. "She isn't your average First Lady."

Anderson brings only a backpack, pistol and a scowl. He constantly tries to find fault with our ideas, and generally undercuts us at every opportunity. He finds flaws with our allies, and I think the only reason he doesn't use the term nigger to describe Thaddeus is out of deference for Crystal.

By contrast, Clause offers as many helpful suggestions as he can. It is his idea to leave Crystal safe at the airport while we go after Matt. He brings a service pistol, bag, and a sword that the Brackley's had, "Laying around for decorative purposes."

When everyone is packed, we reform our convoy. This is phase one of the plan; get to the airport as quickly as possible. The Hummer leads the way again, while the school bus follows. Ackmed and I ride along with Clause, while the others follow. A few zombies are visible, but none seem to notice us as we streak by. Only once are we forced to stop and take refuge in a restaurant called Huck Finns. The restaurant itself is forgettable, and reminds me of any generic diner found in any generic American town. Crystal, however, is impressive. As we run into the restaurant, she blows away two zombies with one blast, then reverses her shotgun in one quick move. Using it as a club, she beats another zombie over the head. When we get into the restaurant, she excuses herself and changes out of her blood soaked sweatshirt as nonchalantly as if she had spilled something on it.

Not your typical First Lady indeed.

Once the horde of zombies tramples past us, we continue to King Thaddeus's Midway Airport. We arrive just before dawn. This time, when we are stopped at the gate, the guards salute us and lead us to Harry Carey's Steakhouse immediately. Over a breakfast of mimosa, steak and eggs, and hash browns, I inform Thaddeus of our plan. Anderson again objects, but Thaddeus and Crystal both overrule him.

Thaddeus likes our plan as well, which is good because it hinges on him.

After breakfast, we are invited to return to our 747 to relax while Thaddeus enjoys some time alone with Crystal. If it doesn't feel like home, the 747 feels at least like a familiar hotel room, and I doze off quickly.

Once my nap is over, we return to Harry Carey's for dinner. Crystal elects to sleep in our quarters after we eat. All of us settle down and go over our specific roles in the plan before retiring to sleep. As we turn out the lights, Anderson argues about keeping a watch until Crystal makes him shut up and go to sleep.

The next morning, an old friend wakes us by banging on the door of the plane. "Wake up White boys," Michael bellows as he enters the cabin grinning like a fiend. Malcolm follows with a confused look on his face.

"Thaddeus wanted to make sure you morons don't get into any trouble, so Malcolm and I are going to go with to keep you safe." As Anderson bristles, Michael bows deeply to Crystal and kisses her outstretched hand. She giggles like a school girl at his gallantry.

We are now ready for phase two. Leaving Crystal and Richard at the airport to get phase three of the plan started, we set off. Despite assurances that she is safe with Thaddeus, Anderson insists that Clause remains with Crystal. Anderson only agrees to accompany us when she makes him. I am hoping that despite his shitty personality, his super power will help us if we need to fight off any of the hordes.

Our journey to the safe house takes only a few hours, so it is still light out when we arrive. Ackmed throws the door open and calls out for Matt, but the late afternoon reveals only eerie shadows in the front room of the house.

Matt is not here.

TWENTY ONE

We wait in the living room, my overactive imagination running in circles. I wonder how long we should wait. Matt should have been here last night, and I can think of no reason that would delay him other than his father catching him. As day turns into evening, none of our group speaks. Every so often, the others look to me for a decision, but I just shrug. Ackmed does not appear to be reclaiming the leadership banner now, so it looks like it will be up to me. As early evening fades into a terrible darkness, I decide that if Matt doesn't appear by morning, we will leave.

The night passes without incident, although this time we keep watch. As the morning sun appears, I gather everyone in the living room for one last meeting. I stand in the middle of the room and say what everyone is thinking. "He's not coming. We tried, but now it's time to-"

I am interrupted by the pop pop of gunfire. I rush to the window, only to see Matt and two others sprinting down the street. "It's Matt."

With a whoop, Ackmed runs outside. He waves his arms and jumps up and down like a little kid. "Matt, we are over here. Hurry up, the house is secure."

It is true. It seems that we were all going to survive this nightmare after all.

When he is about twenty feet away, Matt screams at us. His voice is ragged and he is panting from his run. "It's not zombies. Get the hell out of here."

I look beyond Matt, and I see them. Not a horde of zombies, but a horde of men moving quickly. White men, holding guns. He must have gotten caught.

Pointing to J'Marcus, Malcolm and Michael, Ackmed screams, "Get back about 200 feet and cover us. Then we will run past you and give you cover."

As they begin to move, the rest of us raise our weapons and take aim. Matt and his followers sprint past us, and we fire. The white men stop and most seek cover. They are huge men with beards. Most wear plaid shirts and jeans. It is like we are fighting a logging camp.

Some of the men keep running at us, either braver or stupider than the rest. I have never shot at a person before, and find my hand is shaking. I aim at one man, a youth my own age. He has a red plaid shirt on, which is unbuttoned to reveal a T-shirt with a cross on it. I don't want to kill this man, and I hesitate. Something whistles by my head. It sounds like a bee or fly. I realize that it is a bullet, and that they are shooting at me. My hand stops shaking, and I get angry. They are trying to hurt me. I feel a fire growing in my legs, creeping into my gut. I begin to shake with pure rage. My arms seem like someone else's as I raise my rifle and fire three shots at Red Shirt.

Each shot misses.

If I survive this, I need to take shooting lessons.

One of the men running at us falls. Ackmed grabs my shoulder and yells for me to get back. I run, passing the crude line of our companions behind us. I hear them fire. As I turn around, I see four more bodies on the ground.

I am still angry, but the fire in my stomach disappears when I see the twisted face of one our pursuers. He screams in agony and grabs at his belly. I am angry, but I still don't want to kill anyone. As the others rush past me, I notice that my old foe Red Shirt still follows me. I aim for his legs, close my eyes, and pull the trigger. When I open my eyes, he is lying on the ground, his head a mess of gore.

So much for aiming for the legs.

"Ready." Michael sounds oddly calm about the whole situation. I turn and run again. I hear the evil fly buzzing past me once more, and something nips my heel, but it doesn't hurt so I keep going. I see Malcolm slump and fall to the ground, almost in slow motion. He doesn't move. Michael bends over him, but I am past them now sprinting for all I am worth. When I turn around, Michael is standing in the street firing while the others in his group run towards us. Malcolm still lays on the ground. Michael keeps firing, backing up as he does so. Gradually, the shooting slows and the flies stop buzzing by my head.

"They are slowing down." Kevin shouts to be heard over our guns.

Ackmed nods. "Malcolm, go find a house or something that we can use for cover."

Michael runs up, his Rambo days over. Tears stream down his face, but he doesn't seem embarrassed. There is no time for anyone, even Kevin, to comfort him. He points down the street. "Take a right there, and keep going. We can get to the airport that way."

I nod, and take off for the corner. As I turn, I run headlong into a zombie. I have just enough time to register a short man with a hideous scar on the left side of his face before we both fall to the ground. Pain erupts in my wrist as we fall. I land on top of pretty boy, so I jump up and shoot him in the face, spraying myself with blood and gore.

I look farther east. Pretty Boy had been the vanguard of a horde, which is rapidly approaching. Choosing a house at random, I run in, screaming for the others to follow. I sink into a leather couch, out of breath.

If I survive this, I really need to start working out. Seriously, it's not healthy.

My arm throbs, and I think that maybe I had broken the wrist when I fell. It doesn't matter much now. In a few hours, we can escape this hellhole. The airport is close enough that once the horde disappears, we will be home free. It is sad that we lost Malcolm, but not unexpected. I flex my wrist, reflecting on the sadness of Malcolm's minor character status. In the zombie apocalypse, being a minor character is almost as bad as wearing a red shirt in Star Trek. It is really somewhat of a surprise that we haven't lost more minor characters, although it is too bad that Anderson seems to have survived.

"Malcolm." Kevin sounds somber and upset, like he is fighting back tears. I know that he is compassionate, but Kevin didn't know Malcolm well enough to be upset.

I look up, expecting to see Ackmed looking disapprovingly at Kevin. Instead, he only looks sad. I thought he was supposed to be the cold one, but he looks as if his best friend just died. The others look equally distressed, confusing me further. Malcolm was a minor character. What's the big deal? "I know, it sucks that he got shot. I am sorry."

Kevin points at my arm. "Not that Malcolm. You. Is your arm bleeding?"

I look at my arm, and am shocked to see a stain on the cuff of my shirt. "I must have broken it when I fell."

J'Marcus kneels next to me. "It could be an open fracture. I am going to take a look at it, but if you see your bone sticking out, don't freak, ok?"

I close my eyes. I don't want to see the bone sticking out of my arm. I feel J'Marcus pull my sleeve up. "If I have to set it, it is going to hurt."

I keep my eyes closed. The others in the room gasp. It must look bad, really gross. I am glad that I have my eyes shut. I keep my arm held out, expecting to feel J'Marcus set it. Nothing happens. Opening my eyes, I see everyone in the room, even Anderson, is staring at me with their mouths hanging open. Kevin is crying, literally weeping.

I don't understand. The arm doesn't even hurt that bad. After all that we have seen and done, how could one broken bone be this difficult? Against my better judgment, I look down at the wound.

It doesn't look all that bad. There is no bone sticking out of my arm. There is no great deformity, no mass of flesh exposed to the light. But on my forearm, just above my right hand, a small bite mark about the size of a quarter leaks a steady flow of dark purple blood.

TWENTY TWO

"It doesn't even hurt that much." I try to sound hopeful. If it doesn't hurt, it can't be bad. Maybe it isn't even a bite. Maybe I slipped and fell on some glass or something.

The others look at me, then look at my arm. They draw back collectively, as if I am going to go nuts right away. "It can't be a bite. I can't die."

I can't die. I am the author, the storyteller. If I die, who will finish the story?

J'Marcus stares out the window. His voice is barely a whisper. "I'm sorry Malcolm."

I stare at the wound accusingly. Fucking zombies. Fucking Pretty Boy, with his broken face. I am glad that I shot him, the asshole. And why me? I am a main character. It should have been J'Marcus or Michael. At best, Michael is just a tertiary character in our story. It should be him.

"How long do I have?" I am hoping to see Hester at before I die. I suppose that I can accept my own death, but I would like to hold Hester just once. If there is enough time after that, I would also like to fuck her brains out.

J'Marcus and Michael look at each other. Finally, J'Marcus sighs. Returning to his clinical voice, he explains, "Well you have some time. The wound wasn't fatal in and of itself. You will most likely begin to feel sick within a couple of hours. A fever will develop, and a few hours later…."

"I die." My voice cracks as I realize that I have a few hours left to live. That realization hits me like a clichéd ton of bricks. Even like this, I am a better writer than that. The realization hits me like a semi truck carrying a ton of bricks while barreling down a sharp decline at 80 MPH. At least that is a bit better imagery.

Not that it really matters. Despite my great writing ability, it appears that I am the disposable character in my story. Ackmed and I had been sharing the writing and leadership roles recently, and it is going well. Kevin is recording everything for posterity's sake, and J'Marcus is the group's healer. Matt is our ranged attacker, and Michael is just too damn big to die. He is also black. I said it myself earlier; the black guy always dies. I suppose that I should be happy that my book does not have this trite cliché in it.

If Crystal dies, this whole thing will have been for nothing. That is too depressing. Even though he is a dick, Anderson has a super power. Clause is too nice to die without it being unoriginal. The nice guy always dies.

Richard is needed for the escape plan. Brian and his wife are so new to the story that killing them off would be too easy and meaningless. We don't even know the girls name yet. Besides, a minor character had already died when Black Malcolm was shot.

That leaves only me. A co writer and a bad shot. I am unneeded, redundant. I add another leader to the party, but no man can serve two masters. Fate has decided that the group will follow Ackmed. Here I sit on the couch, a throwaway character in my own novel. It makes me want to weep.

I won't even get to fuck Hester. There is only one woman in the room, and while she is strikingly beautiful, I don't even know her name. Besides, she is married to Brian. I doubt that she will fuck me, even if I say please. I am never going to get laid again. How terrible.

I feel my eyes sting. If I am going to die, I might as well be brave. If I am brave, maybe Brian's wife will at least show me her tits. I search for heroic words. "Well, at least there will be room for everyone in the chopper."

That is phase three of our plan. As we sit in this room, Richard is fixing the chopper that sits in the hanger where we were held by Thaddeus that first night. With luck, it will be ready by the time the others arrive, and they can just fly home.

No one laughs at my joke, and I feel my stomach rise. I know that I am about to cry. Kevin asks how I feel, but I ignore him. The whole room stares at me, and I don't like to be the center of attention. I am- or rather was- a writer. No one pays attention to the writer, because all they care about are the characters in the book. "I think that I need to be alone for a little while."

∎∎

There is a desk in the basement with a computer on it. The computer is a black Emachine, old and slow to boot up. I wait patiently. I need to write, to escape the world for a bit. When Windows finally boots, I open Word and begin to type.

First, I write an ending to our story. A happy ending in which we save the President's wife and sit triumphantly in the White House. An ending where I get to fuck Hester and we all live happily ever after. It is a great story. We end up in Hollywood, where Kevin directs Ackmed in a movie that I wrote. The last scene involves me returning home to my mansion with Hester waiting for me at the door wearing only a trench coat.

But, as Plato said, there is what is, and there is what we would like there to be. And what is right now is that I am dying. I had a cousin that told me once that we were all dying slowly, and I suppose from a certain point of view that is true. But it never really made sense to me until now; I am actually dying quickly. I begin to write, typing my feelings out. It will be important for people to have an accurate description of what goes on in a man's head when he is about to die. As I write, I am forced to break the cardinal rule of writing; I am forced to tell and not show. There is simply not time to compare my feelings to everything. For example, I am feeling hopeful about what will happen after death. It feels kind of like when you are sitting down to a movie that you have seen a great preview for. You hope that the movie lives up to the preview but prepare yourself for it to suck anyway, just in case. I have no idea if there is a Heaven or a Hell. That said, I have seen great previews for Heaven; I hope it lives up to them.

There isn't time for crap like that now though. I can't use cryptic comparisons like that, so I just write that I hope that Heaven is as cool as it sounds. On some level, it bothers me that my last work is going to break every rule that I have ever learned, because I don't want to be remembered as a bad writer.

I finish my analysis, which I cleverly title <u>The Dying Man</u>, and move on to more personal things. I write to my parents, telling them trite things and urging them not to be sad because I am going to a better place. I write a note to Kevin and Ackmed, telling them all the normal things that friends never say to each other. I tell them to think of me every time they play Goldeneye or see a pretty girl.

I write a goodbye letter to Hester. I tell her that I am sorry we will not be meeting after all. It is gallant and chivalrous. I implore her to move on and find another nerd to love. I try to hide my disappointment at not getting to screw her.

I am developing a headache, but there is one more letter I want to write. Opening Word one last time, I type:

Dear Mr. George Lucas:

Thank you for destroying our childhood. Assclown.

Sincerely,

Malcolm Tushton

P.S. Fuck you for the prequels. Learn to write a fucking story, dickhead.

▪▪

As I walk back into the front room, the sun is beginning to set. My headache is getting worse, and my body begins to ache. It feels like the flu, but I know that it is worse, much worse. The group sits around, heads bowed. No one makes eye contact with me. "Thanks for giving me that time. I needed it. "

I hold up a zip drive. "You'll find everything on this. Kevin, you will make sure that they get to the right people, right?"

Kevin takes the disk, then pauses. "Of course. Malcolm, do you want to talk about this?"

"You know that I am more of a writer than a talker. Don't worry, Kevin, I have reached the final stage of grief. It is not hilarity, it is acceptance."

J'Marcus and Ackmed smile, but do not laugh. It was a funny joke, too. Having proven that I am brave enough to go out with a smile, I now need to show compassion to make my friends feel better. "It's not that bad, guys. I am starting to feel sick, so I will make this quick. This was no one's fault, so don't go carrying around survivor's guilt. I have thought about it, and it makes a lot of sense that I am the one out of the group to die. You are all way more important than me. Don't argue it, it's true. I love you all."

The headache is pounding now, and the body aches threaten to knock me over, so I finish my soliloquy with, "Live a long life for me and think of me often. Better friends than these, man has never known. Good luck and God Bless."

I turn and walk upstairs to the master bedroom. My head pounds like a jackhammer. Sorry, another cliché. My head pounds like a construction worker listening to heavy metal with the volume on 10, while operating a jackhammer as his foreman yells at him.

I feel lots of heat. I lay down on the bed, and for a moment it feels cool and refreshing. Then, it grows hot and uncomfortable again. Every neuron in my body hurts as every pain receptor that I have blinks off and on again like a VCR flashing 12:00 after a power outage. The room spins, gets hotter, and spins again. I vomit. As the world turns, I see Kevin's face, sad and crying. Brian's wife picks up a wet rag that transforms into a mass of hot coals. She places the coals on my forehead, and it burns. I scream and beg for death. With the part of my brain that is still lucid, I hope that no one hears me.

I weep for Hester, for the pain, for a young life cut short. And still the whole room spins in a circle, like I am riding the teacups. My body is hot, one massive piece of cooking flesh. The bed changes to a grill, then I am dipped into fire, and that too causes me to scream. I forget what it is to be cool, forget the entire world except for the intense pain radiating from my body.

I see Michael, spinning in circles as he stoically tells me to let go. He changes into Matt, who prays and curses God in the same sentence.

The visuals fade. I no longer see distinct faces, but blurs of color and shapes. This causes me to weep more. Then the fire comes again, and I cry out.

The lights swirl around me, faster and faster, like an ecstasy trip gone horribly wrong. They say that you are supposed to go towards the light, but the lights are so fast and so numerous that all I want are darkness and air.

Between the swirling lights, I see a path of darkness, and I move towards it, letting it envelope me with its coolness.

TWENTY THREE

I open my eyes. The darkness is so deep that I can't see where I am. I know that I am cool and comfortable and laying on a soft surface. I smell body odor, a terrible reeking stench. My head aches and the room spins in slow circles, like a bad hangover.

But my head hurts.

Zombies can't feel pain. If I have a headache, I can't be a zombie. I stand up, but discover my legs wobble like cooked pasta. I fall back onto the soft surface again, breathing heavily. My chest hurts and the room spins faster, like some sort of demented carnival ride. It dawns on me that the soft surface must be the bed, and the terrible smell must be me.

Zombies don't have body odor either. This realization brings a jolt of joy into my brain, but my head hurts too much to dwell on it. The bed is soft and cool, the room is spinning, and as I close my eyes, the wonderful darkness surrounds me.

When I wake again, the light is back. It is not colorful or swirling like the light from before. This is a soft yellow light peaking through the drapes. It must be sunrise. I recognize the room in which I had come to die, if only for the bed. The rest of the room is covered in clowns and stuffed animals. It looks almost cheerful. I lay on SpongeBob sheets that are so caked in sweat that the salt from my body has created white outlines on it.

My legs support me as I stand up. My mouth is so dry that I can barely open it. I walk downstairs to get a drink. I feel weak and shaky, but I manage to find a glass with butterflies painted on it sitting in the kitchen. I put my hand on the sink handle and pause. Do I really want to risk drinking Chicago tap water? The lure of cool water on my lips and cascading into my body makes me decide that it is worth the risk. I turn the blessed water on, but a click interrupts me. I turn away from the now flowing tap, realizing that not only am I thirsty, I also have to pee. Standing behind me, I see Kevin holding a pistol level with my head. His arm shakes, and he is crying.

The gun bobs up and down in the early morning light. "Malcolm, I'm sorry."

I try to smile, but my lips are so cracked that I can't move them. I tell Kevin that I am not a zombie, just plain old Malcolm. My voice is so hoarse from screaming that the words come out, "mdmfmfmrmrfgh."

This reassurance causes Kevin to lower the gun and flee the room, screaming Michael's name. I stumble after him, trying to talk, but it comes out gibberish.

Michael runs up the stairs, cradling his shotgun. "How did he get out of the bedroom?"

I still can't talk. Michael shakes his head, then raises the shotgun. I close my eyes and prepare to die. Luckily, I have practice with this.

The gun makes a clicking sound. "Shit, I never reloaded last night. I'll go get some ammo."

Kevin retreats up four stairs and points his pistol at me again. "Don't move, Malcolm."

His hand shakes again, and he tells Michael, "I can't kill him. Go get more ammo."

Michael disappears back downstairs. Kevin weeps quietly. I shake my head no, moaning. Scanning the room wildly, I notice nothing that will help. There are no pens, paper, or anything at all in the hallway. Michael will be back in few seconds, and I know that he won't hesitate; he had already pulled the trigger once.

I hear Michael approach. The hallway is desolate. There aren't even any pictures, only a yellow light switch. Then, the cliché light bulb in my head goes off. Zombies can't work light switches. I walk over to the switch and flick it on and off as quickly as I can.

Kevin lowers the gun. "What the fuck?"

I try to remember the code for S.O.S., but for some reason the only thing I can think of is the melody for *Message in a Bottle*. I begin to hum as loud and frantically as I can. Zombies can't hum either.

Michael and Ackmed come up the stairs with guns ready. "Why is he humming Sting?"

Ackmed is indignant. "It's not just Sting, it's the Police. There are other band members."

Ackmed loves the Police.

"Whatever. Why is a zombie humming the Police? And what's with the lights?"

"I think that he's sending out an S.O.S. to the world." Kevin begins to hum *Message in a Bottle* too.

I nod my head up and down so vigorously that my neck hurts. I hold up my index finger in the universal sign for wait one second and walk out of the room. In the kitchen, I keep humming so they know that I am alive. The others follow, mouths open even wider than when I was bitten by Pretty Boy.

Stuck on the fridge is one of those pads of paper with a magnet on the back and a pen holder. The paper is blue, with a picture of a shopping cart. Under the words, "Shopping List," someone had written, "Eggs and Milk." Under that, in big black letters, I write, "I am not a fucking zombie. Don't shoot me."

I hand the paper over and take a drink of water. It is cool and clear, and tastes fantastic. My throat seems to shout a thank you to me and the burning stops. I drink another two glasses as quickly as possible. When I cough, I know that I can speak. "Not bad for tap water."

To my immense joy, the words come out, and even though I sound like the grandma from *Dinosaurs*, I can be understood. I fill the glass again and sit at the table, followed by the Kevin, Ackmed, and Michael.

"Why are you not a zombie?" Kevin is always good at asking obvious questions.

I answer in my old lady smoker voice. "I must have immunity, like that guy from Lethal Weapon 2. J'Marcus told us earlier that it was possible for some people be bitten and not turn. Maybe I have the genetic mutation like Anderson. I bet he can explain it better than I can. Where is he?"

"Well, it will have to wait. The others went back to the airport last night. We were going to meet them there once we...." Kevin breaks off, casting his glance elsewhere.

"Killed me? Don't worry, I get it. And I am glad that you are too much of a pussy for that." I smile so he knows that I am joking.

Michael stands up. "Well, no time like the present. Let's get back home."

The journey to the airport is uneventful, but when we arrive at the airport, we discover that Crystal, Anderson, and Clause had taken off that morning.

TWENTY FOUR

"He told us that you were all dead." Thaddeus looks apologetically at us. He sounds generally distressed that he had let the chopper leave. He goes on to tell us that Anderson had limped into camp the night before with a wound to the shoulder. He told Thaddeus that all the others had been killed in a fight with a horde, and that he was the only one that escaped. Urging speed, they had left that morning.

"He must have killed the others, but someone hurt him." Kevin's voice is high, and he has tears in his eyes. He was close to J'Marcus.

I had been prepared to lose one or two more minor characters, just to make the story seem realistic. I thought that Malcolm's death had served that purpose, but apparently Matt, J'Marcus, Brian, and his wife had perished as well. This story is becoming less and less like a thriller and more like an obituary.

When we tell Thaddeus how Malcolm really died, he begins throwing things around his office and screaming. He may be a professorially type, but the murder of one of his men had brought out a mean streak. Between that and the ruse by Anderson, Thaddeus is in a foul mood indeed. After his tirade, he sits calmly down and surveys his ruined office. "I am going to attack those church fuckers tomorrow. With all the stuff you got from the armory, we can destroy them."

Crystal apparently gave everything that we had stolen to Thaddeus in exchange for the helicopter. Anderson must have loved that.

Thaddeus tells us that we are welcome to stay in camp for as long as we want to as honorary black men. We can even attack with him tomorrow. After bestowing this honor on us, he dismisses us with a promise to speak in the morning. He and Michael bend over a map of Chicago and start talking strategy. Recognizing a dismissal, we leave them to their planning.

We stand in the middle of what used to be Midway Airport, in front of a giant map of hat used to be Chicago. None of us want to take part in the attack. Defending yourself against people with guns is one thing, but destroying an entire compound with a gang of black militants is too much for all of us. I don't really want revenge on anyone but Anderson, but without a pilot or plane, there is no way to catch him.

The only revenge to be had will be if we escape and prove Anderson a liar. Staring at the map, Ackmed shakes his head. "But how can we do that? We are on the South Side, about as far from Wisconsin as possible."

"We can retrace our steps out. Once the attack begins, we might be able to get our car back."

Kevin makes a good point, but I want to get out faster. "That will take time, and I don't want Anderson to go public with his story."

In reality, I don't want Hester to think that I am dead. If she becomes upset, she might decide to screw someone else.

Ackmed points at the map. "It sounds like the quickest option. Look at how much ground we need to cover to get out of it otherwise. That could take weeks."

Ackmed begins to tap his hand on the map in pure frustration. His finger is taping the EL station. The Orange Line, to be exact. I notice it. "What about the EL? It's an elevated train, so there shouldn't be many zombies."

Ackmed moves his hand. "It looks like there is a stop about two blocks away, but Malcolm do you know how to drive a train?"

"No."

"A train can only go in two directions," Kevin points out. When we are silent, he continues. "There's got to like a lever or something, right?"

"Look at that map. If we switch lines downtown, we can get on the Green Line all the way out of the city. Once we are in the burbs, we can steal a car and be in Wisconsin by tomorrow night at the latest. " I may be the writer, but Ackmed is definitely editing my work for the better.

We knock on Thaddeus's door and tell him that we would love to help, but we have a train to catch.

■■■

"A train now? What is this, <u>Planes Trains and Automobiles</u>?" Sam laughs at her own joke. It isn't very funny, but she is very pretty, so I laugh too.

"I know, it sounds crazy, but that's what happened." I am grinning from ear to ear like an idiot.

"What?" Her brown eyes stare through me. "What are you smiling about?"

"I was just thinking about what happened next."

"What happened next?" She leans forward, and I look down her shirt briefly before continuing.

"Matt limped up to Thaddeus's office." There is the big reveal. She leans forward even more, and her breasts press against the table. Her cleavage gets bigger.

I continue to stare while I talk. "Needless to say, we were all thrilled that he was alive."

She notices my stare but instead of getting upset seems to flush and smile a bit, the way someone does when they are proud of themselves. "How did he survive? I thought Anderson shot him?"

"Nope, he shot at him. They were walking, and Anderson began shooting them from behind. Matt only had time to spin and fire a quick shot before he ran away. That must be what hurt Anderson, not a zombie. Matt hid out for a bit before making his way back to the airport. He had to avoid all the church people and the patrols of Thaddeus's men in the area." I had looked away when she noticed me staring, but risk a glance again.

"Thaddeus gave Matt the same privileges that he gave us. He was an honorary black man too. When Thaddeus told him about the attack on the Church, Matt chose to go with in order to sort out the good people who were just living with them to survive. Thaddeus said that he would allow them to live, and even help them secure their territory. Effectively, at the ripe old age of 16, Matt became a sort of King."

"So he stayed? With his whole life in front of him?" Sam makes it sound like Matt was an idiot.

"Matt payed attention to the good parts of Church. He had a deep commitment to helping people."

I must have sounded angry, because Sam gets an alarmed look on her face and puts her hand on my leg, which makes it hard to concentrate. "I don't mean it like that. It's such a brave thing to do. So Matt is a King."

"Yep, Matt instantly became a King." I like the feel of her hand on my leg even more than when it was on my arm. I become acutely aware of it as I continue. "We made it to the EL tracks easily, but there wasn't a train there, so we started walking."

● ●

"We are back to being in <u>Lord of the Rings</u>." I know that I am complaining, but no one laughs. It isn't all that funny anyway. Nothing is funny when most of your friends have been betrayed by a bastard Secret Service Agent, so I just keep walking.

It feels surreal to be walking in the middle of the EL track, like I am actually playing *Grand Theft Auto* searching for hidden packages. But, my feet hurt and chilly wind brings me back to reality. J'Marcus is dead. Brian is dead. Brian's wife is dead. Matt is a king, but is stuck in Chicago.

I am resentful of Anderson. Even with the cold and the hurting feet, this trip should be fun. We are heading out of the city, and if all else goes well, we will face very few zombies. Crystal is safe, and we are victorious. This trip out of the city should consist of discussions regarding the top 10 zombie books and top 10 video games of all time. (*Goldeneye* for the Nintendo 64 is still first, by the way.)

Except that it isn't like that at all. The sun is too bright, and we had lost our sunglasses in the truck. It is cold and windy. The city smells like rotten corpses. No one speaks; we just trudge forward, putting one foot in front of the other. The only sound is the dull thud that our shoes make on the tracks.

Anderson has to die. He killed our friends and betrayed our trust. He left us, stranded in an abandoned city, to die alone and forgotten. Six months ago, the idea of tracking down and killing someone would have made me laugh. That was something that characters in books or movies did.

But now it seems natural. Anderson deserves to be punished, by any account. We had been practicing destroying the human form for months. Anderson would be no different, he would just move faster.

Our revenge fueled walk ends with the appearance of the train. It is silver metal that reflects in the bright sunlight and makes me squint. In the last car, a zombie moans and stumbles about, trapped inside. It lunges at us and presses its rotting face against the blood stained window. A sign under the window advertises the Kinect game *Rise of Nightmares*, asking the reader, "Can you survive?"

Heavy handed writing, maybe, but ironic just the same.

The EL train has eight cars, all shimmering in the sunlight. No other zombies stalk around anywhere else. Everyone else must have escaped the train, only to be eaten later.

Ackmed and I squeeze into the conductors booth, which is cramped and built for one person. If I survive this, I should probably work out and lose some weight. Kevin gets in the car behind us and brings out his camera to film the last movie shot in Chicago. There is not just one lever in the train that goes up and down. There are switches, lights, levers, and pulleys. Shrugging, Ackmed pushes one of the buttons.

Nothing happens.

He pulls one of the levers.

Nothing happens.

This continues for about five minutes until the train lurches forward slowly. It clicks and shudders. Ackmed pushes the switch up farther and the engine coughs. The train picks up speed, and we head toward downtown Chicago.

The city flies by outside the window. We pass through the ghetto surrounding the airport and are soon making our way up past U.S. Cellular, where the White Sox play. Soon, we are traveling into the South Loop. The buildings grow bigger and more modern. The south loop had been an up and coming area populated by Actuaries and Attorneys. The neighborhoods are clean and there are nice cars parked outside of buildings. As we enter the downtown area, department stores advertise sales in giant picturesque windows.

A few zombies wander around the narrow downtown streets, but the giant hordes appear to be somewhere else. Most of the zombies appear in the windows of the stores. They stare at us hungrily, chomping and moaning at us.

It is difficult to fathom, but after all this time, seeing zombies seems like an everyday occurrence. If the city had been completely empty, I would be worried; the zombies' hungry stares seem to comfort me, letting me know that I am not alone. Their presence injects some normalcy into our lives.

We round a corner, and all sense of normalcy disappears. In the street, its rear tail crumpled into the side of a building, sits the still smoking wreck of a helicopter.

TWENTY FIVE

The train slides to a stop as Ackmed finds the brake. We are about 100 feet from an EL station. All of us exit the train and stare at the wreckage of the helicopter. Its proud lines have been crushed, and the entire back rotor rests inside a nearby building. Smoke and small flames leap from the wreckage, which is populated by several zombies. They congregate around the shell of the vehicle, ignoring the heat from the flames as they attempt to get inside the wreckage.

"Is that the helicopter they left in?" Anderson may have saved our lives by betraying us.

Kevin, always the scientific one, points out that it is still smoking, so it must be the same helicopter. "Do you think that they are, um...."

"Dead?" Ackmed laughs viciously. "Well something in that chopper is dead because those zombies seem to think that it is a BBQ."

We stand there for a few seconds, watching the helicopter burn and the zombies struggle to enter. A zombie with a blue windbreaker succeeds in falling down and crawling into the chopper. While Blue Man disappears inside the hulk, the others groan in frustration. Ackmed begins to walk towards the station without a word, his head hung low but rifle raised high.

"Where are you going?" Just because this is now a joint venture doesn't mean that Ackmed can do whatever he wants.

Ackmed speaks like a professor in class stating a fact. "We are going to rescue them."

I can't believe my ears. Ackmed, who had never wanted to put us at more risk than he had to, wants to spearhead a rescue attempt. I must be back in charge of writing, because only I could write such a dynamic character.

Ackmed grins like a rogue. "I figured that you would make me go anyway. Besides, this being a hero thing is starting to agree with me. No talk show host is going to want to fuck the guy that almost saved the First Lady."

■■■

Hiding behind a blue Cadillac Escalade, I observe the helicopter from ground level. It is about forty feet away. From the front, it looks almost whole, with only a crack in the glass that Blue Man had crawled through. "It looks like Richard got away, because there is no one in the front seat."

The front seat is indeed empty. So where is Richard? I look around, but see no viable options for escape. The stores, with their picture windows and display cases, teem with the undead. Across the street, the giant window that Macy's decorates every year for Christmas now holds moving mannequins, all hungry for flesh. A baby grand piano, white and shiny, sits on the second floor of the store. Every so often, we hear a musical note being played as one of the undead bump its keys. I would never want to go into one of those stores, but there are no other buildings on the street, and all the surrounding cars are too small to hide in.

That's when I notice the bus. About a block north of us, one of those red double Decker busses, the kind you see in England, is parked. The side of the bus reads "Windy City Tours," in big letters. I had ignored the possibility because a bus is a terrible place to hide. There are too many windows. Then, I see people on the top floor of the bus. They are moving around. Not the jerky, sudden movements displayed by the zombies, but with the fluid motions of the living. We run to the bus and up the stairs to meet the faces of Crystal, Anderson, and Richard.

Ackmed stares angrily at Anderson, managing somehow not to blink. (The alliteration is my handiwork, though, lest you think that in his supreme anger Ackmed has taken over the story.)

"Where's Clause?" Kevin makes it sound accusing.

"Did you kill him too?" Ackmed still hasn't blinked.

If I survive this, I need to have him teach me to go that long without blinking.

"No, he's dead in the chopper." Richard hangs his head guiltily. "We lost all hydraulics. I was lucky to put it down at all."

Richard's head snaps up and he glares at Anderson. "I didn't want to leave without a more thorough checkout, but Anderson insisted we weren't safe at the airport. What weren't we safe from, Anderson?"

Anderson doesn't answer, as he is currently locked in a staring contest with Ackmed.

Richard turns to us. "You look good for guys that got eaten by zombies."

"Reports of our deaths are greatly exaggerated," I reply with a snicker. I have always wanted to say that.

Anderson finally looks away from Ackmed and moves between Crystal and the three of us. "Stay back Crystal. He's infected."

Crystal and Richard look horrified. Richard's bright blue eyes open wide, his face contorting into a frown. "Is that true?"

I don't answer. Instead, I begin my own staring contest with Anderson. I make my voice as cold and emotionless as I can. "The thing is, Agent Anderson, you're not the only one with a superpower."

I roll up my sleeve and reveal the ugly scar on my right arm. "The next time you report that someone is dead, you had best make sure that they are actually dead."

Anderson doesn't speak. Crystal turns to him. She too stares at him, giving him the famous look that all women are capable of employing against men. "You told us that they were killed by zombies."

Anderson has no answer. To his credit, he does not try to hide his actions or make up a false story. "I was trying to keep you safe. They represent a huge security risk."

"Security risk to whom?" That's right, I am so pissed off that I am breaking out the whom on his ass. "We saved you."

"We were doing just fine without you. Then you show up and kill a Diplomat with weapons that you stole from the government. What exactly are your backgrounds again? How could I have known that you or your criminal friends weren't going to use those weapons on us?"

Kevin scratches his head. "Why would we haul our asses all across the Midwest just to do what the zombies were capable of doing without us?"

"Fine, maybe you planned on kidnapping her for ransom. Or using her in one of your sick internet videos. Don't act so surprised. I have heard of you guys, and I know that camera isn't just for documentaries." He turns to Crystal. "Do you have any idea what kind of sick things they have done to people?"

Before she can answer, Anderson continues in a voice that rises to almost a desperate pitch. "Ok, say that they really wanted to rescue you. If we kept chasing every rainbow along the way, eventually they were going to get us all killed. Hell, he did get himself killed. He's just too stupid to realize it."

"So that justifies murdering innocent people?"

"My objective has always been to protect the First Lady above all else." Anderson sounds as if he is quoting from a textbook.

Crystal's eyebrows rise. "Murder?"

Kevin points at Anderson with one hand and begins counting on his fingers with the other hand. "He murdered J'Marcus, Brian, and Brian's wife. And he tried to kill Matt. Don't look shocked Agent Anderson; Matt not only survived, but has been made into a king."

"This is America, there are no kings. You see, Crystal? They and their friends are rebels, traitors to their own nation. A king?" Anderson looks at her imploringly.

She looks at Anderson, her face unreadable. Then, she frowns and shakes her head. "These men just wanted to save their friends. There is nothing wrong with that."

"As for the other things, these are desperate times, and people are trying to survive by any means necessary." Anderson's face brightens, perhaps thinking that his actions have been justified. "Murder is still murder, though, no matter how desperate the times."

Crystal draws herself up to her full height even as Agent Anderson's face droops. When she speaks, she sounds like a judge passing out a sentence. "Agent Anderson, give me your weapon. You are hereby relieved of your duties as an agent."

Anderson laughs almost manically. "Are you going to take me into custody or something? Am I under arrest? The law no longer applies here Crystal."

Before any of us can react, Anderson hits her with the butt of his gun and scrambles down the stairs and out of the bus. He lands amongst a crowd of about five zombies, who snap at him. One manages to bite his shoulder, but he pushes it away and runs to the glass doors of the Macy's. He turns and fires two quick shots at the bus, and disappears inside.

We watch him enter the store before a wall of the dead surround him. He is faster than they are, and therefore stands a chance at escape. After a moment of silence, Kevin points at me. "It has to be Malcolm. He's the only one that can get bitten and keep going. The rest of us won't stand a chance."

It is the truth. I can get bit by the zombies and survive. It will still hurt; blood from Anderson's shoulder wound trails from the street into the store. It reminds me of a grotesque version of the glowing path you follow when playing *Fable*. That path had to be my destination now, because with my superpower I am much like the Hero of Albion. I am special.

That doesn't mean that I want to enter the building, however. As fast as I am when compared to zombies, there is a limit. I could still be killed. I had just gotten over the idea of dying. I want to live. To write. To get rich.

To fuck Hester.

Crystal puts her hand on my arm to reassure me. As serious a situation as this is, I still can't help but notice the heat from her hand, or the way her chest rises and falls under her sweatshirt. Even with blood on her face from Anderson, she is still beautiful. "You don't have to go, Malcolm. He will probably be killed by all those zombies. What he did was horrible, but it isn't worth your life."

I tear my thoughts away from her boobs and think. Perhaps I can get away without going in after Anderson. I can tell myself that he died in that store at the hands of the undead. That is justice, biblical style. An eye for an eye, a tooth for a tooth. Anderson had killed, and would be killed in return. I begin to consider living and just taking Crystal to the train.

One look at Ackmed tells me that if I don't go into the store, he will. His face is set, his jaw is straight. He wants revenge.

I am just beginning to walk down the ladder when we hear the first shot. It sounds far away. Another shot pierces the afternoon quiet. Then another, and another, each one sounding faster and more frantic than the last. The zombies on the second floor near the piano, who up until now had been eying us hungrily, turn away and walk in the other direction.

"You think Anderson is there?" Kevin indicates the building, with its rapidly disappearing crowd. More shots ring out. Through the horde inside, we see a shape that must be Anderson moving quickly. He is running and firing his handgun. He leaps onto the white baby grand piano and fires one last shot, which shatters the window. Then he jumps out.

His face is pure triumph for a half a second. There must have been too many zombies inside to handle, so Anderson had found a way to escape. It must have seemed in that time that he had cheated death yet again. He seems to hang there in the air for a time, face triumphant and arrogant as ever. Then he begins to fall. The look of triumph degenerates into pure terror. Whatever his other superpowers, Anderson cannot fly.

He lands on the ground with a crack. We see the bones of his legs literally snap in half and tear through his flesh, his shins becoming tiny spears poking through muscle, bone, and sinew. Anderson is quiet for a moment, then lets out the most earth shattering, terrified scream that I have ever heard. The zombies surrounding our bus pause and begin to walk across the street to where Anderson lay sobbing.

Those undead would be too late to eat him, however. Already the horde inside of Macy's is beginning to pour out of the shattered window. They fall, and many of their legs shatter like Anderson's, but they ignore the broken bones and begin to crawl towards Anderson. "Don't let them eat me."

He is pathetic, no longer a murderer. He is a trapped, sad animal. There is no hint of arrogance or anger, just a plea. I no longer want revenge on this man.

Kevin moves towards the stairs. "We have to help him."

Ackmed raises his rifle. He doesn't look happy or joyful, and I can tell that he no longer wants revenge either. "I'll help him."

Crystal grabs the rifle just as Ackmed fires. The bullet slaps harmlessly into the back of one of the zombies, who doesn't even turn around as he continues to walk towards Anderson.

"We can't just shoot him. That would turn you into a monster, just like him." Crystal is apparently our new moral compass.

Kevin puts on his metaphorical therapist hat. "She's right. You will regret it. We need to save him somehow."

Somehow is right. There are roughly thirty zombies crawling around Anderson, who is now meowing like an injured kitten. He stretches his arms out at us and pleads for mercy. "Don't let them kill me."

Zombies are still pouring out the broken window and falling to the ground when we hear the first bang. It sounds oddly similar to a big object being moved, but it is accompanied by an odd off pitch musical note. Bang Bang.

Before I can even ask the others what is happening, the white piano falls from the second story window, followed by tons of zombies. The piano falls directly on Anderson, whose screams abruptly end with a musical crash. The piano literally explodes into hundreds of pieces of wooden white paneling, sinewy strings, and broken black and white keys.

Kevin is the first to speak, as usual. "The zombies must have pushed it outside while they were trying to get him."

That's a relief. I thought pianos moved themselves. Richard sighs and shakes his head. "Well, that's justice."

Ackmed opens his mouth. I expect terrible puns to come out. Play me dead. He's playing chopsticks with the devil. But Ackmed surprises me, sounding somewhat sad. "At least he got his wish in the end. The zombies didn't eat him."

TWENTY SIX

"And then we left, and it was over." I spin in my neat leather chair and face Sam, who frowns in confusion.

"You just left?"

"We got back on the train while they were eating Anderson, and drove out into the suburbs. There was only one other incident." I unbutton the top button of my shirt and show her the dark red scar on my neck. "And even that was relatively minor."

"So what about Hester?" Sam's voice goes up a bit. She reflexively glances down at my left hand, which is devoid of a ring.

"We met for a time, but it didn't work out."

She tries to hide her smile by saying, "That's so sad."

"Not really. I think that she was just interested in me because I was far away and inaccessible, and I was just interested in her because I needed a reason to keep going when it got hard." Sam's eyes widen a bit when I say hard. Despite Ackmed's help, I am still the master writer of the group. I hope that this current story will turn into a romance novel or at the very least a session of erotic poetry.

She blushes, but manages to keep eye contact with me. "So, um, did you guys-"

I give her my best Roger Moore smile. "How do you think I got the scar on my neck?"

She looks down and blushes harder. She is cute with a red face. "So what about the others?"

Careful Malcolm. That scar comment may have been too much. Channeling my inner George Lazenbee, I make my voice suitably mournful. "I haven't heard from Matt or Thaddeus. I am not sure exactly what happened to them. Even though logic dictates otherwise, I like to think that they are alive and each leading their respective races in a peaceful cooperative existence."

"I went into the CDC for a couple of months so they could analyze my superpower. I have been poked and prodded in pretty much every hole, and they have needles to make more holes when they run out."

Before I can continue, the door opens and Ackmed comes in with a beautiful blonde on his arm. He looks different than when I saw him last, a bit heavier, but much more relaxed. His eyes don't glitter with as much hate and seem to light up with joy when they see me. He introduces me to the blonde, who turns out to be his new girlfriend, Claire. He had written me while I was in the CDC and told me about his therapy and the new girl in his life. Kevin enters next, talking on his cell phone. He orders someone to do some kind of edit by the time he gets back. He hangs up the phone, and gives me a hug, whispering, "We will talk later, but it's good to see you Malcolm." With that he sits next to Ackmed and asks him how he is doing.

Several men in suits enter the room, followed by Richard, who looks even more ruggedly handsome in a tailored suit. Following him into the room are a couple of old Generals in full uniform with shining medals. They regard us cautiously and sit on the opposite side of the table. Crystal and Grant enter last, holding hands. It is the first time I have seen her in the months since I have been back. She looks completely different from the woman I saw mutilating five zombies in a Huck Finn's. She is now dressed in a classic blue skirt-suit. Her hair is perfectly done, and only a touch of makeup is visible on her flawless face. She has on gold earrings and a pearl necklace. She and Grant walk over to us. He shakes all of our hands and thanks us each profoundly. He apologizes for not meeting with us sooner, but matters of state are matters of state. The implication is that matters of state are far more important than us, which I agree with.

I try not to stare at Crystal too much, even though she is stunning. No one seems to notice Sam but Ackmed, who raises an eyebrow in a silent question.

"Mr. President, they are ready," the General in the blue suit says. Grant nods and the screen comes to life. It shows an image from what looks like Google maps, except that it is moving very quickly. The General hits a button on the speaker phone in the middle of the table and tells us that we are live.

A voice comes in over the speaker. It is clipped, military and professional, with just enough mechanical changes to let us know that it is the pilot. "Red five to Rouge lead, we are nearing the target. Permission to engage."

As part of our deal, I got to pick the callsigns. This is really cool, even if it is also solemn.

Grant says, "Rouge leader to Red 5, engage at will."

"Red 5, vox 2."

Claire squeezes Ackmed's hand. The video changes to a black and white image from the missile heading towards its target. It reminds me of images I saw on TV when I was a kid watching the first Persian Gulf War. The target rapidly becomes clearer as the missile approaches, eventually taking up the whole view screen. I recognize it as Ackmed's house. This is the deal I made with the government. I didn't want any special treatment for rescuing Crystal, but for three sexless months in the CDC, I wanted a reward.

I have just enough time to pick out the fort in the back yard that we used to play in when the monitor becomes fuzzy as the missile hits.

"Red 5 reporting in, target destroyed."

"Great shot kid, that was one in a million." I manage to say it before the General turns the phone off and glares at me. I know that this is a serious moment, but I just couldn't help it.

Through tears, Ackmed thanks me, but tells me that if anyone is Han Solo, it is him. Crystal and Grant shake our hands and invite us all to dinner that evening, which we gratefully accept. They leave quickly, still holding hands. The Generals file out after that, as do the men in suits.

Ackmed and Claire excuse themselves. He tells us that he is grateful and looking forward to catching up later, but he has an appointment with his therapist. Kevin's phone rings, and he answers it as he walks out, telling me that he will see me at dinner.

Sam speaks when we are alone. "So that's that, huh?"

"Yep. It's over."

"So, what are you going to do now?" The tone in her voice makes me wonder if she didn't want to say who instead of what.

"Well, I am going to go put on a nice suit and get ready for dinner." I am playing with her a bit, but I am enjoying my hero status a little.

She looks saddened, as if she is expecting something else. "Ok, I guess I better get back to work."

"What do you think you will wear?"

"Wear?"

I give her my best Sean Connery. "Well, darling, I need a date tonight for dinner with Grant and Crystal."

Sam smiles at me and mutters something in elfish.

I blush again, and look away.

Letter from the author

Thanks for reading my book. I really hope you enjoyed it. This is my first novel, and I have some people to thank before I continue. I would of course like to thank my wife, Janet, who gave me support and listened to me talk about this book for the better part of a year. She even helped perform the final edit. She is a constant source of support, and all of that other sappy stuff that she hates me saying. I did it baby!

In addition, I would also like to thank my mom for encouraging me always to write and express myself. Thank you also for the editing help.

I would also like to thank my friends Derek and Brian for giving me feedback and ideas during this project. In particular, I would like to give credit to Derek for coming up with the idea of the piano falling on Anderson's head. Brian gets the nod for both the cover and various one liners throughout the book. (He contributed a lot to the President's phone call.)

Derek also stole the idea for the diplomatic immunity line from Lethal Weapon 2, and suggested that I put it in. So if the director of that movie is looking to sue anyone, sue Derek.

That's about it. I am planning to write more books soon. Fear not, the gang will be back in a second Zombie Tube novel that I am planning now. I thank you again for reading my book. If you want to drop me an email, feel free.

My email address is Mike@splitscreenentertainment.net. I would love to hear from you!

About the author

Mike Mankoff works as a paramedic, although when he grows up someday, he wants to be a writer. Mike received an English degree from the University of Illinois at Chicago in 2009. His first book, Zombie Tube, appeared in 2012.

Mike enjoys writing sarcastic and fun fiction, primarily horror and fantasy. He lives in the Chicago suburbs with his wife, dog, multiple fish and a yellow bird.

Mike loves hearing from fans, so drop him an email at mike@splitscreenentertainment.net. Also, be sure to check out the blogs he writes at www.splitscreenentertainment.net.